THE DETECTIVE'S SECRET DAUGHTER

Rachelle McCalla

Love Inspired

Thanks and acknowledgment to Rachelle McCalla for her participation in the Fitzgerald Bay series.

Recycling programs
for this product may
not exist in your area.

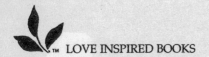 ™ LOVE INSPIRED BOOKS

ISBN-13: 978-0-373-67502-9

THE DETECTIVE'S SECRET DAUGHTER

www.LoveInspiredBooks.com

Printed in U.S.A.

Then you will know the truth,
and the truth will set you free.
—*John* 8:32

To Shirlee, Valerie, Stephanie, Lynette and Terri—
my fellow continuity writers—
and to Emily Rodmell, the amazing editor
who helped us sort through it all. You ladies rock!
I wish we could all meet for coffee and pastries
at the Sugar Plum Café in Fitzgerald Bay.

Acknowledgment

I didn't invent these characters.
Long before I was introduced to Victoria Evans
and her daughter, Paige, or Owen or the rest of
the Fitzgeralds, people I'd never met had already
wrestled over who these characters should be and
where their journeys should take them. Then, in an
enormous feat of trust and courage, they handed
them off to me, and entrusted me with bringing
them to life. To all those who worked together
to make the 2012 LIS continuity the series it is,
I offer my deepest gratitude and humblest thanks.
It is an honor to be a part of these books.

ONE

A police cruiser tore up Main Street in Fitzgerald Bay, lights flashing.

Victoria Evans glanced back over her shoulder from the doorway of the Hennessy Law Office. Who was in trouble now? She half expected the patrol car to stop in front of the police station, but it skidded to a halt on the other side of the street, and a uniformed officer leaped out, running toward the Sugar Plum Café and Inn.

"My shop!" Victoria turned to face Cooper Hennessy, handing off the frosted cookies she'd walked up the street to deliver. "Paige is in there."

"You'd better check it out."

Immediately afraid for her nine-year-old daughter's safety, Victoria didn't need any urging. She leaped from the stoop and sprinted down the street, reaching her front door just as the police officer, who'd darted around the side of the building, circled back to the front.

Victoria reached for the door handle the same instant he did. Gloved fingers brushed her hands. She looked up past the broad shoulders to close-cropped brown hair. The handsome face turned toward her with eyes as blue as the Massachusetts sky. She knew those eyes too well.

"You can't go in there," he warned.

Her heart plummeted to her stomach. "But my daughter—"

"She's okay. She called 911. I don't want you contaminating the crime scene. Wait here." He turned away and rushed inside, leaving Victoria on the porch.

Tumultuous emotions broke like waves inside her heart. She'd already had a crime scene at the Sugar Plum Café and Inn a few weeks before—an ugly break-in that had caused expensive damages. Fortunately no one had been seriously hurt.

What now? Was Paige really okay? Victoria prayed again for her daughter's safety. Having lost her own mother and father years before, Victoria had no family left besides Paige, and the little girl was dearer to her heart than anyone. She had to force herself to follow the officer's instructions not to go inside.

It didn't help who the officer was.

Owen Fitzgerald.

Of all the officers on the Fitzgerald Bay Police Department, why did Owen have to come?

"Mommy!" Blond braids bounced as Paige threw herself through the front door.

"Paige!" Victoria scooped her daughter into her

arms, holding her tight for one long moment before looking her over to make sure she hadn't been hurt. "Thank God you're okay." After the horrible incidents of late, especially after that mysterious murder in January, she was relieved to find her daughter unharmed. "What happened?"

Owen's deep voice answered behind her. "A break-in and robbery. Your safe was punched."

"What?"

Owen led her back through the inn to the kitchen. "Basically your perp knocked the dial off with a hammer, placed a punch over the central hub and rapped on the tumblers. The tumblers disengaged and he opened the door. A newer safe will lock up if anybody attempts to punch it, but these antiques don't have that feature." He pointed across the room to where the Sugar Plum Café's antique floor safe sat gaping open, empty.

"I've been robbed?" Victoria stared at the safe. "I was only gone a couple of minutes. I'd just taken a platter of cookies over to the Hennessy Law Office— barely a block away."

Owen crouched on level with Paige. "Did you see the robber?"

Paige nodded.

"Can you tell me what you saw?"

Victoria's first instinct was to shield Paige from questions. She didn't want her daughter distressed any more than she already was, and she especially didn't want her talking to Owen. He might recognize the family resemblance and realize who Paige was. But Victoria reminded herself that she couldn't let her personal history with Owen interfere with his investigation of the robbery.

Someone had stolen the entire weekend's receipts from the Sugar Plum Café and Inn. And since most of her customers paid for their small purchases of coffee, rolls, pastries and cookies with cash, that money would be irretrievable.

Gone.

Just like her business, if things didn't turn around soon. Fewer folks had been visiting town. And fewer townsfolk venturing out. Partly because of the blustery weather, but mostly due to the ongoing investigation of the murder of Olivia Henry whose body had been found near the Fitzgerald Bay lighthouse in January. Her murder was still unsolved and her murderer still at large. Victoria prayed the case would soon be solved. Olivia deserved justice, and the people of Fitzgerald Bay deserved peace of mind. Hopefully, once the murderer was caught, business would pick up again. With the added burden of repair bills from the recent break-in, Victoria was barely meeting expenses.

The empty safe didn't help matters.

Paige faced Owen.

Victoria braced herself. Paige had never met her father. Owen didn't even know he had a daughter. She'd been putting off their reunion the whole six months she'd lived in Fitzgerald Bay, unsure how she could admit the truth to either of them. Granted, part of her reason for returning to Fitzgerald Bay was so she could clear her guilty conscience and finally do the right thing by telling Owen about Paige. But knowing what to do was easier than working up the courage to actually speak the words to the man who was so much more intimidating now, in his crisp police uniform, with his muscular shoulders and intense blue eyes.

Owen and Paige looked at each other in silence for one long moment—a few seconds that stretched to eternity for Victoria as she considered all that hung in the balance between them. Would they recognize each other? Would some innate father-daughter bond speak to them, giving away her secret?

"My mom wanted me to take the cookies with her." Paige rolled her eyes as she often did when she thought Victoria was being an overprotective mother. "But I already had my pajamas on." Paige looked down at her fuzzy fleece pointedly.

"So you stayed behind?" Owen clarified.

He didn't look up at Victoria, but kept his eyes riveted on Paige.

Did he know? Could he tell? Victoria tried to shake off her fears as Paige continued her story.

"I'm nine years old," she asserted defensively. "I can stay by myself for a couple of minutes."

The words echoed the argument they'd had before Victoria left.

Victoria tensed, watching Owen's face for any sign that he recognized the significance of Paige's age. His jaw tensed. His eyes narrowed slightly. Had he made the connection between Paige's age and their long-ago relationship and realized the truth? Or was he too focused on his investigation? Much as Victoria knew she needed to tell Owen the truth, this was *not* the way she wanted him to find out he had a daughter.

To her relief, Owen seemed focused on being a good cop. "Everyone in town needs to be a little more careful these days," he reminded her gently.

Paige blinked, and Victoria felt a shudder ripple up through her as the little girl leaned more solidly into her arms at Owen's subtle reference to the murderer at large.

Besides being relieved that Owen hadn't jumped at the mention of Paige's age, Victoria was impressed with Owen's perception. She also wanted to set the record straight. "She wasn't home alone. Charlotte is here, somewhere." She looked around the kitchen as though expecting the Sugar Plum Café's hostess to appear any moment. Now where had she gone?

This time Paige didn't roll her eyes. "I came downstairs because my mom told me she left a cookie for me." They all looked to the smooth stainless steel countertop, where a cookie sat undisturbed next to a glass of milk. Victoria had written I Love You Paige in frosting across the heart-shaped pastry, accenting it with silver dragées—Paige's favorite.

"That was nice of your mom," Owen murmured.

Victoria felt him looking at her. She kept her eyes on the top of Paige's blond head. She couldn't meet his eyes—hadn't met them in almost ten years, afraid he'd see the truth that was screaming to get out.

"I came down the back stairs." Paige pointed to the service stairway that opened into the kitchen just behind them. "I heard someone at the back door. That was weird, because Mom went out the front door, and I could hear Charlotte laughing in the dining room under my room, so I didn't know who would be at the back door. It kinda freaked me out and I stopped."

"Smart girl." Victoria planted a kiss on top of her daughter's head, relieved that Paige hadn't walked in on their robber. What would have happened then?

"I tiptoed down the stairs. I thought it had to be somebody I knew. But then I remembered about Olivia." Paige's voice caught. Olivia Henry's death had shocked their close-knit town, and obviously made an impression on Paige, too.

Olivia had come to Fitzgerald Bay from Ireland three months before her murder, not really knowing anyone in town. Since Olivia had stayed a few weeks at the inn, Paige and Victoria, being fairly new to town themselves, had quickly formed a friendship with Olivia that had lasted even when the young woman had gone to work as a nanny for Charles

Fitzgerald, Owen's older brother, who was a medical doctor in town.

Now a lot of folks in town thought maybe Charles Fitzgerald had murdered Olivia. Whether he'd done it or someone else, no one had been charged with the crime, which meant Olivia's murderer was still at large, probably living among them, possibly plotting to strike again. The very thought sent a chill through Victoria as Paige continued to tell the story of her encounter with the robber.

"I stood up on the third step." Paige darted from her mother's arms to the back steps that led up to their private apartment adjoining the inn. Her stocking-clad feet perched on the step as she demonstrated how she'd stayed out of sight. "I peeked around the corner."

"Oh, Paige." Victoria imagined how close her daughter must have come to being seen.

"It's okay, Mom. He was messing with the safe. He wasn't looking at me."

Owen had followed Paige to the doorway and now looked her in the eye as she teetered on the step. "Did you get a good look at him?"

"It was dark. He had his back to me."

"But it was a man?"

"Yes. He was a big guy. He looked like that man—" Paige looked up at her mom "—the one we've seen."

"Outside the windows?" Victoria finished Paige's sentence in a fear-filled whisper.

Though her words were almost too quiet to hear, they sure got Owen's attention in a hurry. "Wait a minute. You've seen this guy hanging around outside your windows? And you didn't call the police?"

Victoria rushed to explain. "It's only been a few times. At first it was a fleeting shadow—we thought maybe it was a trick of the light in the blowing snow. Then we saw him on the porch. But the Sugar Plum Café and Inn is open to the public. People take their coffee out on the porch all the time."

"In March?"

"No." Victoria began to earnestly wish she *had* called the police. "But I don't want to chase off customers. He might have been meeting a friend for dinner. It could have been anything. He didn't seem dangerous."

Owen stabbed a glance at the gaping safe. "From here on out, let's assume he's dangerous." His expression softened when he turned back to Paige. "Did you notice anything else about him that would help us identify him?"

"He was humming."

"Humming?" Owen repeated.

"What was he humming? Did you recognize it?" Victoria had been taking Paige to voice lessons for years, first where they'd lived in New York, then here in Fitzgerald Bay. For a nine-year-old, she had an ear for music and could usually pick up a tune after hearing it only a couple of times.

Paige tipped her head a little to the side. "It was kind of *hmm-hmm.*" She tried a couple of notes and shook her head, obviously not satisfied that she'd gotten it right. "It reminded me of the Irish ballads I've been singing with Mrs. Murphy. Kind of like one of those, but not anything I've learned yet."

"Maybe it will come to you later." Owen pressed on. "What else can you tell us about him? What was he wearing?"

Paige made her thinking face. "A dark jacket and gloves. He broke the safe and took the bag. And then—" her expression twisted and Victoria realized her daughter might be about to cry "—he broke the cookies."

Scooping her distraught nine-year-old into her arms, Victoria patted Paige's back while turning to look at the tall cooling rack where she'd left ten dozen frosted cutout cookies. It had taken her most of the evening to decorate them, between darting up front to wait on the last of the evening's customers and running the register report before tucking the money into the safe. She'd closed at eight—a mere ten minutes ago.

Now the cookies lay smashed all over the floor, clearly stomped upon. Victoria took a step closer to assess the damage.

"Stay back." Owen raised his hand, and his fingers brushed her sleeve. "There might be a decent footprint. We don't want to disturb anything."

Victoria stepped backward, not needing physical contact with her long-ago beau added to her evening's troubles. Her heart stuttered at the faint touch of his hand. Was it her imagination, or was he even more handsome than he'd been in high school?

"What's the fuss in here?" Charlotte Newbright's plump figure entered the room, and she gasped as she stared at the gaping safe, its locking mechanism collapsed in on itself. "We were robbed?"

Owen turned to the older woman. "Have you been in the building for the last ten minutes? You didn't hear anything or see anyone?"

Charlotte's dyed red hair in its choppy, gold-streaked cut fluttered as she shook her head. "I was in the northwest dining room, chatting with your brother Douglas and that pretty little Merry of his. Such a darling couple." With that pronouncement, Charlotte planted her hands on her hips and turned to Victoria. "Everything was in the safe already, wasn't it, dearie? You ran today's report just before you left."

"Yes. The whole weekend's receipts," Victoria tried to stifle the deluge of emotions that threatened to overwhelm her. "We were too busy for me to make it to the bank Saturday morning. Friday through Sunday were in that safe."

Owen looked up from his notepad. "You'd already cleared out the cash register, even though Douglas and Merry were still here?"

"Oh, yes." Charlotte waved her hand, answering for

Victoria. "We close at eight on Sundays, you know, and they were the last ones here. When I asked them if they wanted dessert, they knew it was close to closing time, so they paid for their meal before I brought them their pie. Told them to take as long as they needed. Got to talking with them—such sweet folks."

Victoria realized Charlotte might jabber on infinitely if she wasn't interrupted. Her friendliness was an asset to the Sugar Plum, especially since Victoria preferred to stay in the kitchen, but the woman didn't always know when to stop talking. "I'd just totaled out the cash register before I left to take the cookies up the street," she clarified.

"I see. So all the money was in the safe. Can you tell me what was taken?" Owen asked.

Victoria squeezed her eyes shut. Yup, she could tell him exactly how much, but that didn't mean she wanted to speak the words out loud, in front of her daughter and Charlotte, who would only worry.

"Let's get you up to bed, Paige," Charlotte suggested. "It's almost bedtime."

"But my cookie—"

"You can bring it upstairs."

Paige's eyes brightened and she consented to going upstairs with Charlotte. Victoria felt a rush of relief, glad Paige was leaving the room before Owen recognized anything of himself in her, or caught on to the significance of her age. As long as he didn't find out when Paige's birthday was, he likely wouldn't make the connection.

As the two headed for the door, Owen cleared his throat.

Victoria tensed, fearful he'd ask Paige a telling question.

But his words were innocent enough. "Is my brother still here?"

"They left just before I came into the kitchen." Charlotte shook her head. "I locked the front door after them. I'm sorry we didn't see you come in or he might have come back to see for himself what was up, him being the police captain and all. But those two wanted a booth in the back corner, out of the way and to themselves. Didn't even bring that little boy of hers with them, and you never see Merry without Tyler." She gave her tongue a meaningful cluck. "That's serious romance, if you ask me, getting a babysitter and all."

"Thank you," Victoria whispered to Charlotte gratefully. "Good night, Paige. I'll be up to tuck you in shortly."

"Take your time," Charlotte said with a wink.

Victoria wasn't sure what the wink was for. Because Charlotte was removing Paige from the potentially traumatizing crime scene? Or because she was leaving Victoria and Owen alone? Charlotte had her own ideas about Victoria's need for a man in her life, but Victoria had made it clear she wasn't interested in romance.

"Paige?" Owen called her back before she reached the steps. "Can I ask you one more question?"

Paige turned back to Owen, patiently looking at him with eyes so much like his—because they were his. Fitzgerald blue eyes.

"When is your birthday?"

"January 10."

"And you turned nine this year?"

"Yes."

Victoria worked up the courage to look at Owen. His attention was on Paige, and though he kept a kind smile on his lips, his blue eyes had hardened.

"I'm sorry I missed it by almost two months. Happy birthday, a little late." He dismissed her with a wave, and she carried her cookie happily up the stairs with Charlotte huffing along behind her.

Owen stared after the little girl as she disappeared from sight.

She couldn't be.

She *had* to be.

Was Paige his daughter? Owen flipped to the calendar at the back of his notebook and counted off the months. Nine months before January 10 would have been April 10. Ten years before, he and Victoria had been together until mid-May.

His head swirled and he tried to think. Victoria had

left him, running off with Hank Monroe right after graduation. Paige was Hank's daughter. Everybody knew it.

Except the calendar indicated otherwise.

Owen shook his head. Focus. He had to focus on the investigation. Ever since Olivia Henry's death two months ago, the Fitzgerald Bay Police Department had fallen under intense scrutiny. Folks claimed they'd bungled the investigation of Olivia's murder. People were demanding answers, afraid there was a killer loose among them.

He couldn't yet answer the question of who killed Olivia Henry, but he could investigate this break-in with a straight head, even though questions about Paige's paternity rose like bile in his throat.

Victoria had stepped around the center island. Was she trying to avoid him?

Determined not to bungle anything, Owen turned his attention to Victoria. "Can you tell me what was taken?"

Victoria looked across at the safe as though envisioning what had been inside less than half an hour before. "A red bank bag—the First Bank of Fitzgerald Bay. It contained all my receipts for the last three days."

"How much?"

"This weekend was the best I've done since—" she swallowed "—since Olivia was found. Almost three thousand dollars. Only about five hundred of that was by credit card. The rest was cash or checks."

Owen studied her face as she stared at the open safe, either transfixed by its emptiness or else stubbornly refusing to look at him. The top button of her white chef's blouse was open, and he could see a vein throbbing madly, indicating she was frightened. Of the robber? Or of him?

The date on the calendar taunted him, and in spite of the year clearly printed at the top, Owen's thoughts rushed a decade back in time. His life had been turned upside down in an instant. His cousin had been killed by Victoria's father in a car accident, and Victoria had left town without contacting him, though they'd been seriously dating at the time. He'd tried to reach her, to let her know he didn't blame her for what her father had done, but she'd left before he'd been able to find her, and soon the rumors had started flying.

Victoria wasn't the only person to leave town abruptly after graduation. Hank Monroe had left, too, and the rumor was that Hank and Victoria had run away together. Owen had wanted to deny it, but then Hank's father, a respected judge, had told him to his face that it was true. Victoria had only been using him to make Hank jealous. She'd gotten her man. She had no more use for Owen.

For ten years, Owen had tried to convince himself that he was over Victoria, that the only feeling he felt toward her was anger. She'd used him and left him without so much as a goodbye. And now, if the nine months between April and January and Paige's Fitzgerald-blue eyes were any indication, she'd stolen something even more precious than his heart. She'd taken his daughter.

Victoria couldn't look at Owen. Had he guessed the truth? She forced herself to keep talking about what had been stolen from the safe. "That might sound like a lot of money, but most weekends I don't make a fraction of that much, and midweek business is slower still. By the time I pay my employees and cover my costs for food and heating…" As she thought about her expenses, Victoria found herself feeling overwhelmed. She'd needed that income.

But God had seen her through plenty of tough times before, raising her daughter alone on one income. God had provided her with a flexible pastry chef position in New York City, and through that had taught her what she needed to know to run the Sugar Plum. Victoria believed God used everything in her life—even the difficult times—as ingredients for the recipe He had planned for her life.

But what good could God possibly bring from the broken safe and missing funds?

She shook her head. "I needed that money."

"I'm sorry." Owen's words carried emotion, not the formal just-the-facts-ma'am voice he'd been using thus far.

For a second, Victoria was tempted to meet his eyes, to feel that human connection he offered in the sympathy in his voice. But she'd been head over heels in love with Owen when they were in high school. In the six months she'd been back in town, she had yet to spend any time around him. She'd seen him, of course, coming and going from the police station across the street, and her heart had always done a mad dance at the sight of him.

Because she dreaded telling him the truth? Or because she still had feelings for him, even after all these years? Until she was certain those feelings were gone for good, she didn't want any traitorous emotions sneaking up on her—not with the confession she still needed to make. After all, Owen had every reason to hate her. It had broken her heart to leave him the first time around. She wasn't eager to find out how upset he might be when he knew the whole story.

She felt fear rising in her heart and, hoping for a distraction, she turned to look at the ruined mess of cookies on the floor. The few that weren't broken were a lost cause, anyway, never mind that she kept the floor spotless.

Owen must have seen where she was looking. "And the cookies?"

"Ten dozen. They sell for a dollar fifty each, or three for four dollars. It's less than two hundred dollars lost revenue—"

"But your time…" Owen tapped his pencil against

his notepad. "The bank bag I can understand. That's a lot of money. It makes sense to steal that. But the cookies—what would anyone have to gain by breaking your cookies?"

Victoria looked at the crumbled mess as though she might find the answer there. The sight of the broken cookies, each one a heartfelt labor of love—some of her customers even called them works of art. Why would anyone destroy something so innocent?

"Do you have any enemies?"

"No." Victoria cringed at his question. The closest thing she had to an enemy was Owen himself. How would he feel when he learned she'd hidden his daughter from him all these years? He would hate her. And yet, she knew she had to tell him. Her heart beat hard inside her, and she could feel a recreant blush rising up to her ears.

"Are you sure?"

It was an invitation to tell the truth, to be released from the secret that had burdened her ever since the day almost ten years before when she'd learned she was pregnant and wondered whether she should tell him. But her father had crashed his pickup into the car driven by Owen's cousin two days before that. Patrick Fitzgerald had been killed instantly. Victoria had run away to New York to stay with her father's sister. It had taken her almost ten years to work up the courage to return to town. She didn't have the nerve to admit the shameful thing she'd done by hiding Paige from Owen all these years.

"Not anyone who could have done this."

Owen stared at Victoria's face. Why wouldn't she look at him? His heart burned inside him with ferocious fire. Was the blue-eyed little girl who'd gone upstairs his daughter?

"Victoria?"

She looked up about as far as his chin. He wished she would lift her brown eyes a little higher so he could try to read the truth there. But then, he could see the truth in the color of her daughter's eyes. Victoria's eyes were brown, but Paige had blue eyes—Fitzgerald blue eyes, just like his.

"Hank Monroe has brown eyes. You have brown eyes, but Paige…"

Victoria's chin quivered. "I came to Fitzgerald Bay to tell you the truth."

Owen felt his stomach plummet. Was she saying what he thought she was saying? "You've been in town six months, and you haven't spoken to me. Hank Monroe's been going around claiming Paige is his. Were you aware of Hank's claims?"

"Yes."

"And you've never denied them?" Owen had always scoffed at the suggestion that he'd inherited an Irish temper, but something was charging through his veins with fury. He wanted the truth, and he wanted it ten years ago.

Victoria's voice cracked and broke off in a whisper, "I thought you should be first to hear the truth."

TWO

Owen gripped the stainless steel island countertop. He wasn't sure what was more upsetting—what Victoria wasn't saying, or the fact she wasn't saying it.

"Is Paige my daughter?"

"Yes." Victoria's voice broke to a whisper and she covered her face with her hands.

Rather than rip the countertop from the island, Owen let out a long, slow breath and willed himself to calm down.

He had a daughter.

"You hid her from me for ten years?" Anger hurled his words at her.

"We came back—"

"You know how important family is to me. How could you—"

She looked up at him with terrified eyes, and he let the question die unspoken. He was a law enforcement officer, sworn to keep the peace and uphold justice. There was nothing to be gained by shouting at

Victoria. What if Paige heard him? What if he frightened his own daughter?

"Does Paige know I'm her father?"

Victoria shook her head. "I hoped that, by moving back to Fitzgerald Bay, she might get a chance to know you. That might make it easier when she learns she's your daughter."

He had a daughter.

Anger fought with doubt and betrayal and disbelief inside his heart. He needed to sort out his feelings before he spoke to Victoria anymore. He needed to talk to a lawyer. But that wasn't going to happen tonight.

In the meantime, he had a robber to catch. And he had a job to do, if he was going to keep his daughter safe. He schooled his voice into something reasonably civil. "I'll take a look around back and see if I can find any footprints. The perpetrator was gone by the time I ran around the side of the building. But then, Paige told the dispatcher she'd waited for him to leave before trying to use the phone."

Victoria looked as though she wanted to say more, but she seemed to take her cue from his mechanically forced words. "How soon can I sweep up the cookies? I'll need to get to work on another batch."

Owen studied Victoria's face—it was easy enough to do, since she refused to look at him. How could she be worried about cookies when he had a daughter upstairs, who'd seen the robber who'd punched the safe?

How could she do anything as mundane as sweeping the floor, when his world had just been rocked to its core?

He wanted to punch something, but instead Owen crouched to inspect the trampled crumbs, putting himself through the motions of investigating. There were no clear footprints, no residue that might point to who had smashed them or where that person had last been. One perfect cookie teetered on a pile of broken crumbs, a bright green frosted frog with buggy eyes and a cheerful smile. He lifted it carefully.

"You can have that."

"Hmm?" He looked up to see Victoria standing by with a broom and a dustpan.

"You can have that cookie if you want it. The floor is clean, but I can't sell it now."

He didn't want a cookie. He wanted the past ten years back, but he couldn't have them.

He took the cookie. "Thanks. You can sweep those up. I'd check the safe for prints, but if he was wearing gloves, as Paige said…" He let his voice trail off as he stepped out of Victoria's way, and she immediately set to work sweeping.

The woman never stood still. Even in high school, she'd been in constant motion, a full schedule of classes, constantly taking care of her father since her mother had died when she was younger, and when she wasn't busy with that, baking.

Always baking. When they'd dated, she'd insisted

on bringing goodies over for the whole Fitzgerald clan. He'd suspected she was trying to win the affection of his family, but then she'd left him for Hank and never looked back, so perhaps he'd been wrong about that. Perhaps he'd been wrong about a lot of things concerning Victoria. He'd never dreamed she would do something so heartless as to steal his own daughter and hide her away from him.

He had to focus on the investigation and swallow his emotions. People claimed the FBPD officers had let their emotions toward his brother Charles color their perception of his potential guilt in Olivia's murder. Owen couldn't let his personal life get in the way of his police work. "I'll check with Douglas after I'm done out back. Find out if he noticed anything."

"What do you think?" Victoria's eyes stayed on the cookie crumbs filling her dustpan. "Will you be able to recover the money that was stolen?"

Owen hated giving her a grim prognosis. "We have Paige's description—" which fit plenty of men in Fitzgerald Bay, his own three brothers included. "We'll see what we can do."

"So in the meantime, what am I supposed to do?" She seemed to be forcing her words to stay steady, but Owen could hear a rising note of panic underneath.

"Do you have cash reserves? A fund set aside in case of emergency?"

"I did. But the break-in last month caused extensive damage. The repair bill was huge—new windows, a new door. I still haven't replaced the bedding and pillows that were ruined."

She didn't come right out and say it, but Owen understood. The Fitzgerald Bay police were failing her. She'd experienced far more than her fair share of trouble, and it was getting expensive.

"We'll find this guy," he told her, wondering how he could ever keep his promise. The solve rate on a theft like this one wasn't good, especially considering the circumstances. But what else could he do? At the very least, he had to keep Paige safe. "And we caught the guy who broke into Detective Delfino's room last month. He'll have to make restitution for the damages."

"I know." Victoria dumped the colorful crumbs into the trash. "It's just taking a while. And it was so nice to finally have a strong weekend."

"You know, my grandfather set up a community foundation years ago. They have grants available. You might try applying for one."

He watched, waiting for a response, as Victoria put away her broom and dustpan. Then she turned her back on him and entered the walk-in refrigerator without so much as acknowledging what he'd said.

Owen stared at the stainless steel door through which Victoria had disappeared. For a second, he thought about going into the fridge after her. If anyone had a right to walk out on the conversation, *he* did. But he was at least trying. *She* was the one who'd wronged him by hiding his daughter from him all these years. What gave her the right to walk out on a conversation with him?

Granted, the woman was shaken. She'd been robbed. He'd seen plenty of folks get upset over a lot less than three thousand dollars, so he figured she was entitled to react however she wanted. She was holding together pretty well, all things considered.

But the woman had a thing for leaving, for walking out. She'd left town with Hank Monroe right after graduation, never even properly breaking up with him first, or telling him goodbye. And now she wouldn't even stick around when he was trying to help her?

The stainless steel fridge door didn't budge, its mirrorlike surface distorting the confusion on his face as it reflected back his image. Did Victoria hate him? If anyone had a right to hate anybody, he figured he was the one who'd been wronged. If anything, Victoria ought to be begging his forgiveness.

He snapped his notebook closed and headed for the back door. If the perpetrator had left any footprints, he'd find them. He'd stick to the things he could control—the steps of the investigation. And somehow he'd sort out what he needed to do about Paige and Victoria.

Victoria retreated to the back of the walk-in fridge and slumped against the silvery door that led to the freezer. Her knees weak, she slid to the floor, unable to hold back her tears any longer.

She'd done it. She'd admitted the truth to Owen.

Now she needed to pull herself together so she could check on Paige and make sure she wasn't too shaken up by what she'd seen. If her little girl saw her like this, she'd only be frightened more.

Wiping back her tears, Victoria sniffled and looked at the refrigerator magnet she'd inherited from her mother, which she kept in the fridge as a daily reminder of her mother's faith.

The truth will set you free.

"I told him the truth," Victoria whispered, trusting God to hear her. "I finally told Owen the truth." She took a deep breath, waiting for the exhilarating feeling of freedom to rush upon her.

No feeling came, except nausea as she thought about the injured look in Owen's eyes. She had never meant to hurt him. Never in a million years would she have purposely hurt him. But there was no way to take back what had happened, Patrick's death or the past ten years.

On the night of her father's accident, when her aunt had taken her away, Victoria hadn't yet learned she was pregnant. She wouldn't have left without telling Owen, if she'd known. But her father's offense stood like an impenetrable wall between her and the Fitzgeralds. There was no way she could face any of them after that.

Her hands trembled as she pulled herself to standing and contemplated all that had happened. Her safe had been robbed. Her daughter was frightened, and Owen…

Owen had looked mad enough to tear the counter-top right off the island. Bless his heart, he'd always been so determined to prove that he didn't have an Irish temper. But she had once known him well, as well as she'd ever known anyone, and she could see the fury brewing just below the surface.

Sniffing back the last of her tears, Victoria put on a brave face. She'd comfort her daughter, bake some more cookies and make back the money that had been taken. She had a business to keep afloat and a daughter who depended on her. She didn't have time for tears.

Owen checked the property thoroughly before heading back across the street to the police station. He rounded the corner to the office he shared with his fellow police officers, and stared at Hank Monroe's desk.

Hank, of course, wasn't there. His shift had ended as Owen's began. But Owen glowered at the desk just the same.

Had Hank been lying all this time about Paige being his daughter? Or worse yet, did Hank not know Paige wasn't his?

The realization churned in Owen's gut. Of course, that made more sense. Hank was an officer of the law, sworn to uphold the truth. He wouldn't knowingly spread false rumors.

Owen quickly put the facts together. Six months before, when Victoria had returned to Fitzgerald Bay more than nine years after she'd left, Hank had told Owen that he was hoping to work things out with Victoria. Hank had gone so far as to imply that he also hoped he and Victoria would be getting married and living together as a family.

But Victoria said she wanted Owen to be the *first* to know that Paige was his, not Hank's.

Which meant Hank didn't know.

With an ominous feeling in his gut, Owen looked at the picture on Hank's desk, of Hank and his father, Ronald Monroe, an esteemed retired judge. Though Hank wasn't the nicest guy, he valued family just as much as any of the Fitzgeralds. Had he hung his hopes for a family on Victoria and Paige?

What would happen when he learned the truth? Would he hate Owen?

One thing was certain: though he wasn't looking forward to Hank's disappointment, Owen had to make sure his fellow police officer wasn't kept in the dark any longer. He'd have to confront Victoria and make sure she let Hank know the whole truth.

As she chopped her way through the lunch specials the next day, Victoria couldn't help taking out some of her frustrations with every slice of the knife, mincing shredded lettuce extra thin and slamming down her cleaver on sandwiches with enough force to rattle the butcher-block surface of her sandwich prep counter.

It wasn't just the shadowy figure who haunted her store, or the robbery and the knowledge that she'd have to put in a banner week just to make payroll. Victoria couldn't help chafing at Owen's reaction to her confession.

She'd known he'd likely be upset. That was why it had taken her so long to work up the courage to tell him the truth. But he'd been so closed-mouthed about it. Didn't he believe her?

Sure she'd heard the rumors circulating around town that Paige was Hank Monroe's daughter, and the wild claim that she and Hank had run off together after high school. The idea was absurd! She couldn't stand Hank Monroe—never could. Surely Owen knew her better than to think she'd let Hank get that close to her.

But now what? She'd told him the truth. She felt as if she was waiting for the gavel to drop.

Slam! Slam! She sliced through a red onion with her favorite knife, slid two rings onto a bed of lettuce and added a pickle. "Order's up!"

Britney, her fresh-out-of-high-school waitress, picked up the plate. "I'm off early today," she reminded Victoria. "I have that appointment at one-thirty."

"Five more minutes?" Victoria had to make six

more sandwiches before she could leave the kitchen and cover Britney's half of the café. By then the lunch crowd would be easing, and even if it didn't, Victoria wasn't about to complain. She needed the business. God knew how much she needed it. If she made enough to cover payroll this week, it would be an answer to her prayer, bordering on a miracle.

But God had seen her through plenty of tough times in the past. God had gotten her through single motherhood with a colicky infant, through car troubles and money troubles until she'd turned twenty-five and received the money from her parents' life insurance. And then God had shown her to use the money to buy the Sugar Plum Café, just as her mother had always wanted to do.

Victoria held tight to the hope that God would see her through her latest trials, though she couldn't see how.

Six sandwiches later, Victoria washed her hands and took over ringing up the tickets Britney had been sure to distribute before she'd left. Fighting to open a roll of quarters, she didn't even look up as the next customer approached. "Can I help you?"

"I'd like a Reuben sandwich." Deep voice. Broad shoulders.

Victoria glanced up and immediately wished she had a good excuse to run back to the kitchen. At least it wasn't Owen Fitzgerald this time.

No, it was Hank Monroe, one of Owen's fellow

police officers, the other name at the top of her list of people she didn't want to see. When she'd rejected Hank back in high school, he'd gotten his revenge by telling everyone that they'd slept together. It seemed he'd let rumors of Paige's paternity persist as a way of backing up his juvenile story.

But she wouldn't let him bother her. Not today. She was leaning on God alone today.

Victoria totaled his order and reached for the money he held out to her, hesitating when she saw the number in the corner. "Our policy is not to break hundred-dollar bills."

"Keep the change."

Victoria looked at Hank. She tried to shake her head, but it ended up as more of a tremble.

Hank leaned on the oak edging that bordered the large glass pastry case. "I heard you could use the money."

It took a moment for Victoria to sort out what Hank must mean. Right. She'd told Owen she needed the money that was in the safe. Hank and Owen both worked for the FBPD, but not on the same shift, obviously, since Hank was in uniform right now, probably on his lunch break, and Owen had been working the evening before.

Had Owen been talking to Hank? What else had Owen told him?

"I'm sorry." Victoria took the bill and quickly counted out Hank's change, slapping twenty-dollar bills on the counter emphatically. "I don't know what you're talking about." She scooted his change toward him.

He pushed it back. "Victoria." His voice rumbled with something. Impatience? Warning?

She didn't like it. "Let me get your sandwich." Leaving the money on the counter for him to take, she spun around to the kitchen, washed her hands and quickly assembled the Reuben he'd ordered.

"To go?" she asked as she slid the wrapped sandwich into a small sack, hoping he'd take the hint and go.

A glance at the money on the counter told her their conversation wasn't over.

Hank grinned at her.

Victoria grabbed the cash and stuck it in the sack with his lunch. "I appreciate your concern, but the rumor you heard is incorrect." It didn't matter how tight things got. She wasn't going to sink to taking handouts, especially not from Hank Monroe, a guy who never did anything nice without expecting something in return.

She shoved his lunch toward him, wishing she could as easily shove him out the door.

Instead of taking the bag from her, he placed one gloved hand over hers.

She tried to let go, but his grip was surprisingly strong. Customers sat just beyond them in the first dining room. They could see everything that was happening—could even overhear their conversation if they listened closely enough.

Embarrassment worked its way up the back of her neck. "Hank." She tried to infuse warning in her tone. What was Hank up to? Had Owen upset him?

"I'll keep the change if you let me take you out to dinner," Hank countered.

Memories surged up—memories that had been buried even deeper than her long-ago relationship with Owen. She'd gone out to dinner with Hank once, eleven years before. Never again. No dinner, no matter how nice, was worth what Hank had wanted for dessert.

Wriggling her fingers from his grip, she managed to yank her hand away. The sack went flying and money spilled out.

At the same moment, the bell on the front door jingled and a customer walked in.

Hank's wrapped sandwich hit the floor, along with several large bills and a clatter of coins spilling from the sack.

Victoria's stomach plummeted. How many people had seen? She dared to glance up at the customer who'd entered.

Owen Fitzgerald.

He'd seen the money.

"Is that your lunch, Monroe?"

Hank Monroe scooped it up. "It is."

"That's awful rich eating for lunch."

Victoria wanted to reach behind her and pull the oak pocket doors closed, to block the view of the scene from her customers in the dining room. But she couldn't turn around. Couldn't face them.

"Victoria and I were just making plans," Hank said. "Dinner. Somewhere nice."

"That sounds good. I'm sure the two of you have plenty to talk about." Owen glared at Victoria as he spoke. Though his tone was soft enough on the outside, probably for the sake of all the customers within earshot, his words were shot through with icy shards of pure spite.

Mad enough to throw both of them out of her store, Victoria explained in a low voice, "Hank heard somewhere that I was low on cash. He kindly offered to increase my reserves. But I'm not that desperate."

As she spoke, Hank turned and headed out the door.

Victoria wished that Owen would follow him, but instead the off-duty officer addressed her softly. "You need to tell him."

"Tell him what?" Victoria spoke softly through gritted teeth. "*You* already told him I needed money."

Owen held up his hands. "I haven't talked to Hank—"

"Then who did he hear it from? How many people have you told?" She stomped back around the glass pastry case.

"No one."

Victoria shook her head. "I'm not that stupid."

"Neither am I. How long do you think I'd make it

on the police force if I blabbed the details of every case to everybody?"

Her frustration boiled over. "I didn't realize the Fitzgerald Bay Police Department had performance standards."

Owen gave her a look that was pure malice. "We do our jobs."

"Do you? I'm located right across the street from the police department, and I've had two terrible break-ins less than a month apart. Why can't you keep me safe?"

"You do your job and I'll do mine." Owen planted his hands on the counter. "I want a turkey melt with extra avocado. And a cinnamon roll."

"Anything to drink?" Anger seethed just under her words.

"Milk."

While Victoria rang up his purchases, Owen leaned toward her, his voice quiet. "Look, I'm just here to talk to you about your robbery. I'm not going to discuss…"

Victoria gave him his total, waiting as he pulled out some cash. "You're not going to discuss *what?*" Her heart slammed inside her chest, but she was upset enough she didn't care.

"Paige," he whispered.

Almost as though he couldn't bring himself to speak his daughter's name out loud.

A horrid sense of guilt washed over Victoria, the same shameful feeling she'd so resented when strangers had looked down upon her as an unwed teenage mother. She'd hated that feeling, but it was worse when Owen was the one making her feel that way. "Okay." She counted out his change. "The robbery, then. What about it?"

"I was thinking about the narrow window of opportunity the perpetrator had to commit his crime. Who knew you were going to be stepping out?"

"Just Paige and Charlotte."

Owen's low tone was almost conspiratorial. "You mentioned delivering the cookies to the Hennessy law firm. Who was there at that hour?"

"Cooper. I think he must work late a lot. They have a standing delivery of cookies on Sunday nights, and whenever I call over to arrange the delivery after we close up at eight or nine, Cooper's usually still there."

"What about Burke?" Burke Hennessy was Cooper's father, the patriarch of the Hennessy clan and the founder of the Hennessy Law Office.

Victoria shook her head. "I've never seen him there in the evening. You don't consider him a suspect, do you?"

"They knew you'd call before bringing over the cookies."

"But he's a lawyer. I'm not saying that makes him honest or dishonest, but you don't think he'd stoop to stealing, do you?" As she spoke, Victoria opened the back of the glass case to fetch the cinnamon roll Owen had ordered.

"I don't know if monetary gain was necessarily the primary motive." He tapped on the glass, pointing. "That caramel one in back looks great."

Victoria pulled it out with a pair of tongs. "Then what do you think was the motive?"

Owen leveled his gaze at her, and this time she couldn't help but meet his eyes. Clear blue, and piercingly intent. "I'm going to ask you again—do you have any enemies?"

A shudder rippled through her, and she bit back the words *only you.* Her voice trembled slightly. "I didn't think I did."

"Well, I believe you do now."

"Who?"

"That's what I intend to find out. In the meantime, I think you need to be careful."

"You think they might strike again?"

Owen nodded solemnly. "Paige is very lucky she wasn't seen. I'm afraid I may have given her the wrong impression with my questions. I don't want her to think she needs to try to get a look at this guy if she sees him out the windows again. She made all the right choices, but I'd like you both to take extra precautions in the future. Talk to her about safety. Or if you'd rather, I can talk to her."

"I'll talk to her," Victoria hastily reassured him.

"Good. And call the police if you even suspect something might be off. We're right across the street. It's no trouble. I'd rather stop in a hundred times for nothing than…" He let the implied danger go unspoken as he took a step back for a customer approaching, ticket in hand.

Victoria nodded. She understood. They were in danger. She had an enemy—nameless and faceless though the man was—and she didn't know when or how he would strike next.

THREE

Owen clutched the white paper bag that held his lunch and walked outside into the crisp March air. His breath hung like a white cloud in front of him, as ephemeral as the wall of denial he'd tried to put up since the night before.

Paige was his daughter. Ignoring that fact didn't change anything. Much as he needed time to digest the new reality, at some point, he knew he needed to act on what he'd learned—but not before Hank knew the whole story.

Staring at the police station across the street, Owen almost wished Hank would step out so he could tell him to talk to Victoria. But Hank was nowhere to be seen, and if he was honest with himself, Owen wasn't certain what his role was regarding the relationship between Hank and Victoria. Convinced as he was that Hank needed to know the facts, Owen felt a tiny shimmer of doubt. Maybe Victoria had a reason for not telling Hank everything. Maybe there was more to the story than he knew.

But he wasn't going to stand still and let Paige continue to grow up without him. Owen headed down the street to the Hennessy Law Office. Though the law office made it a practice of offering free cookies every Monday morning, Owen hoped he could catch Burke or his son alone.

When Owen stepped in, the offices looked deserted, save for a picked-over platter of cookies and the last of a pot of coffee on warm. But Owen heard the sound of typing through one of the open doors beyond and called out, "Good morning!"

Cooper trotted out. The fair-haired man, just a few years younger than Owen, greeted him. "Detective." He nodded a greeting. "What can I do for you this morning?"

"I need some legal counsel."

"Right this way." Cooper ushered him back to an office. "My father's not in right now—"

"That's all right. I'm sure you can answer my questions." Owen took a seat in the visitor's chair. Never having been one to mince words, he let the confession spill out. "I just found out I have a child."

"Infant?"

"She's nine."

"Paige Evans?"

Owen froze.

"I'm sorry, it's not my place—"

"No, you're right, Cooper. How did you know?"

"She looks like you. And back in high school, well, that would have been about the right time—"

"I was under the impression that everyone thought Hank Monroe was Paige's father," Owen said.

"That's what I'd always heard."

"Have people been saying otherwise? Has anyone suggested…" Owen felt a rising sense of panic. What if Cooper wasn't the only person in town who'd guessed at the truth?

"No, no." Cooper held out his palms as though to physically squash any rumors. "I'd never heard anything of the sort—hadn't even thought about it myself until you said she was nine. Paige comes over with her mother most Sunday evenings when they make their cookie deliveries. She mentioned having a birthday a couple of months ago, turning nine. I just put the two together."

Owen caught his breath, poised to get on with the legal questions he needed to ask, when a feminine voice called from the back of the offices.

"Cooper?"

"That's my stepmom." Cooper went to the doorway. "Christina."

The forty-something woman jangled in, her kitten heels clacking on the floor, glittering baubles dangling from her earlobes, neck and wrists. She held a wriggling one-year-old at arm's length. "Cooper, can you watch Georgina? I have to do some shopping, and the nanny took the day off." The woman's glossy lips pouted slightly.

"Sure." Cooper smiled at the tot, who lunged for him as she was handed over. "Can she have a cookie? They're from the Sugar Plum."

"That's fine. She had an early lunch." Christina handed over a patent-leather diaper bag with quick instructions on the little girl's care. Cooper nodded as though he knew the drill.

Owen watched in fascination, marveling at Georgina's chubby hands as she explored inside Cooper's shirt pocket, pulling out a pen and nearly stuffing it in her mouth before Cooper caught it and swept it off to the safety of his desk, leaving Georgina babbling insistently, wanting it back.

So that was what his daughter had looked like at one year old. He'd missed that stage. He'd missed two and three and four...all the years up to nine, and he was missing that, too.

The anger he'd been fighting down began to rise again. Victoria had stolen all those precious years from him, all the chubby-fisted, toddling, baby-talking experiences that were integral to parenthood.

Christina excused herself quickly and Cooper settled Georgina in with a cookie and some playthings he apparently kept in a basket under his desk for just such occasions. "Sorry for the interruption, Owen. Now, your daughter—"

"Yes. Paige." Owen finally realized exactly what he

wanted to ask. "I need to find out how to attain parental rights."

"Visitation rights?"

Owen did the math in his head. Victoria had gotten the first nine years. Paige would graduate from high school in nine more. He had to take what he could get. "Joint custody."

Eight o'clock. Victoria watched the hand on the large grandfather clock creep toward an upright position. It was dark outside, and she found herself jumping at every shadow. What if their robber came back? What if he was lurking outside this very moment?

"I'll get the tables in the back dining room." Paige swept past her, cleaning cloth in hand, and Victoria felt tempted to stop her.

The back dining room was around the corner, out of sight from the front counter. The last customer had already left, and Victoria was busy closing out the register and totaling the Tuesday receipts. She wouldn't be able to keep an eye on Paige.

It bothered her. Much as she wanted to trust God to keep her daughter safe, she didn't want to be foolhardy and invite trouble. Besides, Paige didn't need to help out so much.

For the past two days Paige had been eager to be extra helpful, but Victoria wasn't sure why. Had she caught on to how strapped they were for cash? Victoria didn't want her daughter growing up with those kinds of concerns on her shoulders. That was the way Victoria had been raised—first worried about the expenses of her mother's illness, then the toll of her father's drinking. She knew how stressful money concerns could be to a young child who didn't even understand financial affairs. No, she wanted her daughter to have an innocent childhood.

She hurried to count out the cash so she could check on Paige, keeping her ears pricked up to the distinct patter of her daughter's feet against the floorboards.

By the time Victoria zippered the cash safely into a brand-new bank bag, the long hand on the clock had moved into an upright position. Finally, they could close. The day had been a grueling one, and all the uncertainties she'd been dealing with of late only made her feel that much more exhausted, and eager to get the doors solidly locked. She headed toward the front door, keys in hand.

"Mom?"

Victoria nearly jumped. "Yes, Paige?"

"He's back."

"Who?" Victoria asked, though from the fear in her daughter's voice, she knew exactly whom Paige was referring to. The shadowy figure—maybe the same guy who punched their safe.

"The bad guy, outside the back dining room—I saw him through the big picture window. I don't think he knows that I saw him."

Victoria shoved the bank bag into the waistband

of her pants and grabbed the cordless phone from Charlotte's hostess podium. "Where's Charlotte?"

"I don't know. But it wasn't her. It was a man."

"Did you see his face?"

"No." Paige took the phone that Victoria pressed into her hands.

"I'm going to take a peek. You stay right here. Be ready to call 911." Victoria tried to look casual as she crossed through the front dining room to the large back dining hall. She didn't want to scare the intruder off, not if they were going to have any chance of catching him. But she also had no intention of calling the police if it was just Charlotte outside—though why Charlotte would be outside on this blustery March evening, Victoria couldn't imagine.

Straightening the napkin holders on every table, Victoria worked her way toward the big picture window, head down, eyes surreptitiously up. There was a fire exit out the back corner of the room, an emergency-only door that was always locked.

Or at least, it had been locked every time she'd checked it, for so long that she hadn't checked it in a while.

The skin prickled on the back of her arms.

Was it her imagination, or did she hear something brush against the door?

Her eyes riveted on the antique brass knob. For the first time, she wondered if the inn's antique appointments she'd once found so charming were really such a good idea. A modern safe would have kept her money from being stolen. Was the antique doorknob going to betray her, too?

The doorknob rotated a fraction of a turn and stopped with a click, then turned back the other way. Another click.

What should she do? Victoria was torn between throwing open the door or running the other way.

"Paige," she called out in a voice that was meant to sound casual, though she could hear fear screaming through it. "You can place that phone call now."

Her ears pricked up. She could hear the faint tones of the dialing phone. But closer and somehow louder, scratching at the emergency exit door.

From the entrance, she heard Paige's trembling voice answering the dispatcher's questions. "The Sugar Plum Café. The bad guy came back. I saw him outside."

Victoria could imagine the dispatcher's side of the conversation, but she prayed the woman would stop asking questions long enough to send an officer over. And preferably not Owen Fitzgerald this time.

Another scraping sound came from the doorknob. Was someone trying to pick the lock? She watched with wide eyes as the knob began to turn. Again a smidgen to the right. A click. And now to the left, but this time, it turned and continued to turn.

Unsure whether to run or stand her ground, Victoria felt frozen by fear. Surely it wouldn't take long for an officer to arrive. The police station was right across the street. But what if all the officers were out on patrol? What if they arrived too late?

The doorknob continued to turn. Had someone picked the lock? Were they going to make it inside?

She heard the sound of the front door opening. Thank God she hadn't locked it yet.

"Thanks, he's here." Paige's voice echoed through the front hall. "The back dining room."

Victoria watched the antique doorknob turn and the door begin to ease inward. She braced herself for the sight of whoever might be on the other side. The reassuring sound of heavy boots strode across the oak floors behind her. An officer.

"Blustery cold, blast it all." Charlotte Newbright's voice surprised her a split second before the back emergency-only fire exit door opened all the way, revealing the spiky red hairdo of the hostess.

"Charlotte!" Victoria sagged with relief.

"Charlotte?"

Victoria didn't have to turn around to recognize the voice of the responding officer. Why did Owen Fitzgerald always work the evening shift?

Charlotte closed the door behind her and stomped her boots on the floor. "What's all this now?"

"We received a phone call—" Owen began.

"Did you see anyone out there?" Victoria asked with urgency. What if the shadowy figure was still lurking around?

"Someone?" Charlotte shook her bright hair and re-locked the door. "Just that stray cat that's been hanging about. Chased him around the side of the building from the back kitchen door. Didn't feel like trudging all the way back around after a chase like that."

Victoria realized Charlotte was panting. The round woman was easily winded, and her story made sense. Sure, Victoria had seen the stray cat plenty of times in recent weeks, but she hadn't given it any more thought than she had the shadowy figure. "You have a key to this door?"

"I don't use it much." Charlotte had worked for the Sugar Plum long before Victoria had bought it. The woman knew all sorts of things about where items were kept, which floorboards creaked and all manner of details about the place that Victoria was still learning.

Paige had entered the room and sidled up against her mother. Victoria put an arm around her daughter. She was glad no one had been hurt, but at the same time, frustrated that they hadn't come any closer to catching the robber.

"What caused you to think Ms. Newbright was an intruder?" Owen asked.

Victoria spun around to face him. She wanted to remind him that he'd told her to call at the first hint of danger. He'd put them all on high alert.

But Paige spoke first. "I saw someone outside the window. It wasn't Charlotte. It was a big man—just like the big man who broke the safe." She crossed her arms over her chest. "I know what I saw."

"Perhaps when Charlotte chased the cat around the building, the intruder ran off before anyone saw him." Victoria didn't come right out and say it, but she was fairly certain the cat would have had a good lead on Charlotte, allowing plenty of time for the man to retreat. She placed a comforting hand around her daughter's shoulders.

Owen must have realized he'd offended Paige, because he crouched down to her eye level. "Did you get a better look at him this time?"

Paige wrapped her fingers around Victoria's arm. "He looked like the same guy. I was scared. I came to get my mom. Do you think I should have tried to get a better look?"

"No!" Victoria wanted the robber caught, but not at the risk of endangering her daughter. "You did the right thing by coming to get me, Paige. I'm glad you didn't get any closer."

"Your mother's right." Owen nodded. "We don't want you to put yourself in danger, Paige. I'm going to take a look around outside. The ground is frozen, so there probably won't be any footprints, but I'll see what I can find."

"Thank you. I'm going to lock all the doors behind you."

But Owen raised a hand as if to stop her. "I'll come back in and discuss with you what I find."

Victoria was tempted to argue with him, to suggest that there was nothing more to discuss, but she had some questions of her own—questions she didn't want Paige overhearing. Her daughter had been frightened enough. The little girl didn't need any other worries keeping her up at night.

Owen stomped the hard earth in frustration. The cold weather wasn't helping his investigation. Not only did the firm ground resist the impression of footprints, but the freezing temperatures had everyone wearing gloves—eliminating the chances that he might find fingerprints on the windowsills. March had certainly come in like a lion. Hopefully it would go out like a lamb. Maybe then he'd get a break—or at least some traceable footprints.

He turned toward the front entrance to the café in disgust. At least he'd get a chance to talk to Victoria.

His discussion with Cooper the day before had been enlightening. While the young man had sympathized with Owen's desire to make up for the nine years he'd missed, he had warned him that attaining joint custody of Paige wouldn't be easy, especially considering that he had no relationship with her and hadn't contributed to her care in the past nine years.

But the fact that Victoria had hidden Paige from him was one item solidly in his favor. From what he'd observed so far, she was a loving mother. But he deserved a chance to be a loving father.

The front foyer of the Sugar Plum was a wide, gracious room, with its quarter-sawn oak woodwork and the glass pastry case nearly emptied of treats by the day's customers. Owen closed the door behind him and studied the room, as though answers might be hiding anywhere, if only he could open his eyes wide enough to see them.

Victoria's stocking-clad feet made almost no sound as she descended the floral carpet runner that graced the antique staircase. "Find anything?"

"No. Is Paige okay?"

"She's in bed reading. I think she's more upset by your questions than she is afraid of the robber." Victoria sighed. "And I guess I'd rather have her angry at you than frightened for her safety."

Though he didn't like knowing he'd offended the sprite, Owen was glad, for Paige's sake, that she wasn't overly terrified, either. "I didn't mean to offend her."

"She's nine, going on nineteen. Sometimes you can't help but offend her." Victoria reached the bottom of the stairs and looked up toward him, her warm brown eyes scanning the room, but never quite meeting his eyes. "I'm sorry if we called you over here for nothing."

"It wasn't nothing. I agree with your theory that Charlotte may have sent the man running. The question is, what was he doing here?"

Victoria shivered visibly. "I was thinking about that. Maybe you know more about this, but I always thought Fitzgerald Bay was a peaceful, sleepy little town. Part of the reason Paige and I moved back was because I wanted her to have the same upbringing I did—in a small town, with good schools, where everyone knows everyone else and people watch out for each other."

Owen heard the yearning in her words, and it echoed his own feelings. It was what he'd always wanted for his family. "Fitzgerald Bay *is* a peaceful town. It's just lately, since Olivia's murder, all sorts of problems have been cropping up."

"That's just it." Victoria wrapped her arms around herself, not so much in a defensive posture, but as if she was trying to comfort herself. "Do you think it's only a coincidence that all these things have been happening all at once? Or is there something bigger going on here?"

Owen felt the hairs at the back of his neck stand on end at her words. After several years in police work, that didn't happen to him often. "What do you mean?"

"I mean, what if it's connected? What if this bad guy is after something Olivia left behind? Maybe the robbery Sunday night was just to cover up what he's been up to. You were wondering why he would break the cookies. It doesn't fit the profile of a robber who just wants money. Maybe he's not after money."

Snapping open his notebook, Owen jotted a couple of notes.

Victoria continued. "And the break-in last month—

in Detective Delfino's room. That was the same room Olivia stayed in when she first came to town."

"But that break-in was related to an old case Nick had been working on back in Boston, not Olivia's case."

"Are you sure of that? Olivia's murderer is still out there, and lately it feels like the Sugar Plum has become a target. I'm just trying to sort out why." She hugged herself, one hand wrapping securely around the bank bag Owen had spotted tucked into her waistband earlier.

"Is that your bank bag?"

She nodded.

"What are you planning to do with it? You haven't replaced your safe yet, have you?"

"I ordered a new safe, but I'm not sure how long it will take to arrive. I thought I'd put this under my pillow tonight and deposit it as soon as the bank opens in the morning."

The jolt of fear Owen felt for her safety surprised him. He told himself he wasn't as much concerned for her safety, as his daughter's. Surely the feelings he'd once had for Victoria had disappeared when she left town. "That's not a good idea. You put yourself in danger that way. If anyone wants the money, they have to go through you."

"But I have to keep the money safe." Victoria looked up at him with challenge in her eyes.

Like a flashback from the past, the look on

Victoria's face reminded him of all the times they'd gone head-to-head when they'd dated ten years before. He'd loved the way she'd challenged him—making him fight for his side, whether it was the sports team he rooted for or what movie they were going to see. But the stakes were higher now. Owen buried the swirl of emotions that threatened his objectivity. "You can't put yourself at risk. I can take the bank bag over to the police station for tonight, but you need to figure out a solution until your safe gets here. You can't put yourself in danger."

He watched Victoria wrestle with the decision as she slowly pulled the bag from her waistband. For a second, he thought about how he might try to convince her if she turned him down again, but then he caught himself. Victoria had wronged him. So why did he feel the urge to wrap a comforting arm around her? He'd loved her once, very much. And it would be far too easy to let his feelings for her resurface. He couldn't let her big brown eyes distract him. He was on duty, and the officers of the FBPD had a reputation to rebuild. Though he wanted to talk more about Paige, now was not the time.

Victoria placed the bag in his hands, and relief washed over him. "I'll keep it safe," he promised, forcing himself to keep his thoughts on the case, even when her hands brushed his, sending a jolt to his head. He couldn't forget that someone had broken into the

Sugar Plum, and his daughter's safety was at stake. "I didn't find any cat prints."

"What?" Victoria's eyes widened. "What are you suggesting?"

"I don't know. It's entirely possible that Charlotte chased a cat through the backyard, but then again, Charlotte isn't known for running after anything she doesn't have to. Why chase the cat all the way around the building? Why not just scare it off or call animal control?"

"Maybe she wanted to see where it went."

"Maybe she was meeting someone," Owen said.

"What? Who?"

"Charlotte knew the money was in the safe Sunday night. She knew it was a big take."

"But Charlotte has worked for the Sugar Plum for decades. She was the hostess here when my mother was the pastry chef twenty years ago. She loves this place."

Owen nodded. "And she tried to buy this place before you did, but she couldn't afford it."

"So you're suggesting she'd steal from me, put me out of business and then use the stolen funds to buy the store?" Victoria shook her head. "I trust Charlotte."

"And I trust the people of Fitzgerald Bay. But as long as we're considering suspects, let's not disregard someone who had both motive and opportunity. And if she had an accomplice, she'd have the means, too."

"That doesn't make her guilty."

"No, but someone is. And I don't think you're going to like finding out who it is."

FOUR

Owen looked up at the sound of a knock on his office door.

Victoria stood in the doorway with a platter of cookies in her hands, the expression on her face one he recognized from years before, whenever she was unsure of herself. Come to think of it, she'd looked that way every time she'd ever been to the Fitzgerald family home, usually bearing treats as she did now.

He joined her in the doorway. "Did someone order cookies?"

"These are a gift." Victoria extended the platter toward him. "To apologize."

"For?"

"My behavior the other day, for one thing. I was very rude. And also, well—" She peeked past him into the office, as though worried about being overheard. She looked relieved to see that no one else was in the office, and she took half a step farther in. "I owe you more than a platter of cookies, I know. But I thought it would be a start." She handed over the tray.

"I'm not going to turn away your cookies—" Owen chose a cheery frosted yellow duck "—but you were perfectly justified in feeling frustrated. Our department owes you answers and action. You've had more than your fair share of trouble lately. We've failed you, and I'm sorry." He took a bite of cookie as he finished, but his eyes didn't leave her face.

She still had that fearful expression, as though she might bolt at any moment. "All this time, I was so worried about how you'd take the news about Paige." She looked up at him, her wide chocolate-brown eyes rimmed by thick lashes he'd once found so beguiling. Maybe he found them beguiling still. "But I haven't heard from you, other than when you showed up to investigate our intruder the other night. I thought, well…"

Owen listened with guilt churning in his gut. He knew exactly why he hadn't been by—because he hadn't sorted out his feelings yet. And because it had occurred to him that he hadn't been around a nine-year-old girl since his little sister Keira was that age. The prospect was more than a little intimidating.

"The reality of the situation is still sinking in," he admitted truthfully.

"I just thought you'd be more curious." Victoria looked lost—as lost as he felt. "I know it's been almost ten years now, but I feel like I owe you my side of the story. Don't you want to know what happened after graduation?"

Owen's gut twisted a little more. He didn't want to dredge up the pain of all he'd lost, and the last thing he wanted to hear was her reasoning for leaving him and running off with Hank Monroe. He had to work with the man on a daily basis, but he was nearly certain whatever Victoria had to tell him would change the way he looked at Hank. "Can't we leave the past in the past?"

Victoria's mouth dropped open, but before any words came out, Ryan Fitzgerald, Owen's oldest brother and the deputy chief of police in Fitzgerald Bay, carried an open box through the office door.

"Owen, take a look at this." Ryan set the box on Owen's desk, next to the platter of cookies. "Are these your cookies?"

"Help yourself." Owen poked open the cardboard flaps of the small box.

"Is that a baby blanket?" Victoria asked.

"I believe so." Ryan lifted the blanket gingerly with one gloved hand. "This package just arrived in the mail. By the looks of the postmark, it was mailed yesterday from the Fitzgerald Bay post office." With his other hand, he plucked up a small pale object with tweezers.

"What is *that?*" Owen asked.

Victoria stared at it.

"Is it a hospital bracelet?"

"It's awfully small to be a bracelet—" Owen began, but Victoria shook her head.

"It could be a baby bracelet. That would make sense with the blanket." She circled around the desk, but stopped short of looking over Ryan's shoulder. "I suppose it's not my place—" she began.

"It sounds like we could use your expertise." Owen peered over his brother's other shoulder at the small band. "Henry Baby Girl," he read quietly, and his eyes scanned the rest. It was dated a little over a year before, with what looked like a time, 22:47, and then "Dr. O'Rourke."

"Henry Baby Girl," Victoria breathed from her vantage point over Ryan's opposite shoulder. "The only person with the last name Henry—" She looked up and swallowed.

"Olivia," Ryan finished what all of them were thinking.

"Did Olivia have a baby?" Owen asked, still unsure what to make of the contents of the box.

"If she did, she never told me. Maybe the baby belonged to a relative with the same last name," Victoria suggested.

"Then why would this package come *here?*" Ryan shook his head.

"What about Meghan Henry?" Owen snapped his fingers. "She's Olivia's cousin. She shares her last name—and she's certainly within childbearing age. Maybe the baby was hers."

Ryan looked skeptical. "If these belonged to Meghan, she would hold on to them, don't you think?

There's no reason for anyone to send them to us. I'll ask Meghan, but my gut instinct tells me this is related to Olivia's murder. Why else would they be delivered here?" He turned to Victoria. "If I'm going to follow up on Meghan, I might as well check into any other members of the Henry family who these things could have belonged to. Did Olivia ever mention any other family members?"

"Not to me, and I was as close to her as anyone, except of course for Merry." Merry O'Leary had been Olivia's closest friend, and had unfortunately been the one to find Olivia's body two months before. Now Merry and Owen's older brother Douglas were seeing one another after working together closely on the investigation.

Ryan shook his head. "Merry has shared everything she knew about Olivia. She's as determined as anyone to solve her murder. She wouldn't have left out a detail like this."

"Maybe the baby wasn't Olivia's then." Owen finished off the duck cookie in his hand. "If that's a birth date, the baby would only be a year old now, and younger when Olivia first came to town. That's a pretty current memory to never mention to anyone."

"Unless she had a reason not to mention the baby," Ryan suggested.

"A secret baby." Victoria sounded as if she was still coming to grips with the revelation. "Poor Olivia. What do you think happened?"

"Do you suppose the baby died?" Ryan wondered aloud. "The loss might have been too painful for her to discuss."

"That sounds plausible," Owen agreed. "Why else would a person never mention their child?"

Victoria scowled down at the bracelet. "Maybe she was hiding her daughter—maybe she was afraid if the baby's father knew about her, he'd try to take her away." She gasped. "Maybe he already did take the baby away."

"You think she was kidnapped?" Ryan asked.

"Or won in a custody battle."

"Preference tends to go to mothers in those deals," Owen pointed out. Cooper had already briefed him on the statistics when he'd been by his office two days before.

"Yes, but what if he was from a wealthy family, someone of means and an established reputation, and she was just a poor single girl with nothing to show? Olivia mentioned that she was raised by just her mother, who died of heart disease a couple years ago. She and I had that in common—both losing our mothers. If she had no support network, no income, the baby might have been given to the father. That would explain why Olivia came here—to get away from painful reminders of her child."

Her words sounded heartfelt, and Owen had to remind himself to deal with the facts of the case. Victoria wasn't talking about her own child, but Olivia's. Wasn't she?

"Your theory would certainly fit the circumstances," Ryan agreed. "I'm going to search for this Dr. O'Rourke and find out if he can tell us anything about the child born on this date. He should be able to tell us for certain who the mother was. The hospital will have records of the birth—including the father, if one is listed, and they would know if the baby died, especially if it happened early on, maybe even shortly after birth."

"Oh, poor Olivia."

Victoria's words tugged at Owen's heartstrings. He reminded himself that Victoria was a compassionate person. Her response had nothing to do with her own situation. They were discussing Olivia's daughter, not hers. He had to focus on the case. "Is there anything else in the box?"

Ryan gingerly sorted through the lightweight blanket. A small piece of paper fluttered out, landing in plain sight on the desk.

A check. Made out to cash. Signed by one William Sharp, who, from the looks of the information on the check, was an attorney in Manhattan. The check was dated a few days after the birth date on the bracelet.

Victoria let out a tiny gasp. "It was never cashed. Oh, poor Olivia. Do you think this reinforces my theory?"

"It certainly coincides with it," Owen admitted reluctantly. "But the father may not have won the baby. He may have paid for custody."

"Is that legal?" Victoria asked, her expression appalled.

"Perhaps in certain circumstances." Owen shook his head. "Not likely, though."

"Do you think this might be related to Olivia's death?" Victoria pressed.

"Of course," Ryan answered.

"How can it be?" Owen asked at the same moment.

"What do you mean?" Ryan asked.

"She didn't cash the check." Owen pointed to the slip of paper that rested on the desk. "It doesn't make sense. If she came back and asked for more money, then I could understand her being killed to keep her quiet, but how could she ask for more money? She never touched the first ten grand."

Ryan twisted his mouth into a thoughtful expression. "But there's more going on here. This package was mailed from Fitzgerald Bay. Somebody here in town had these items. How could this *not* be related to her death, then?"

Victoria's face scrunched up as though she might cry. "Doesn't it all make sense? She didn't cash the check. She didn't want the money. But he killed her." Victoria swallowed back a cry. "He killed her because she wanted her little baby girl back." Her fingers shook as she lifted them to her mouth, stilling her lips, which trembled.

Owen observed Victoria's emotional reaction. What was it about Olivia's story that had Victoria reacting so strongly? Was it because they'd been friends? Or did Victoria know more than she was telling? She certainly sounded convinced of her own hypothesis about what had happened.

"We'll catch him," Owen said, the conviction in his voice surprising, even to him. "We'll catch whoever did this. We will bring Olivia's murderer to justice."

But Ryan shook his head morosely, clearly confounded by the new, mystifying elements of the case. "Don't make a promise you can't keep." He faced Victoria. "I'd be obliged if you didn't speak about what you've seen in here today. We'll try to sort out who might have sent this package and what it means, but in the meantime, any knowledge we have that isn't public may be our only advantage."

Victoria's eyes widened. "I suppose I shouldn't have seen what was in the box."

"I'm glad you did." Owen rushed to reassure her that her presence hadn't been a nuisance. "You've provided valuable insights. You knew Olivia better than either of us ever did. Olivia was a female with a daughter. So are you. That means you can understand her in ways Ryan and I can't. In fact, if you think of anything else—something Olivia might have said that didn't seem important before, or any new connection on why she might have come to Fitzgerald Bay, of all places, or who might have mailed this box—"

Victoria nodded eagerly. "I'll call you. Right away. Olivia deserves justice. And her baby—" Victoria stopped, and her mouth trembled slightly "—her baby may still be out there, somewhere." She looked down at the Manhattan address on the check. "Possibly with her mother's killer."

Owen exchanged looks with his brother. The game had changed. They weren't just working for justice for the dead, but for the living. There was a missing baby out there somewhere.

As Victoria stepped through the doorway, she looked up at Owen with the same wide-eyed expression she'd worn on her arrival, and he realized their conversation about Paige had been interrupted.

He debated what to say. Should he offer to talk with her again? He still wasn't sure he could sit through a conversation without being overcome by the feelings that raged inside him. But then again, if he wanted to learn anything to help him attain joint custody, he needed to know more about Victoria's relationship with her daughter.

"Is there a time we could talk?"

She looked relieved that he'd asked. "Sometimes business is slow in the afternoons. You could stop by then." She looked up at him through those long eyelashes, and suddenly he was a teenager again, dropping her off at her father's front door, hoping for a good-night kiss.

He shook the thought away. "I'll be by then, if I get a few minutes."

A faint smile flitted across her face, and she fled back down the short hallway.

Owen watched her go, a thousand questions still storming through his mind. What was it about Victoria that made his heart beat with such a funny rhythm? He was angry with her—furious that she'd taken his child from him. And yet, at the same time, there was a part of him that still wanted to pull her into his arms.

Ryan cleared his throat, and Owen turned to find his oldest brother watching him closely.

"Well, that explains it." Ryan's eyes narrowed with distinct displeasure.

"What?"

"I looked at your file on the Sugar Plum incidents."

"And?"

"I'm wondering…" His brother's mouth seemed to take its time working out his words. Odd. Ryan usually had no trouble stating his mind. "Are your feelings for Victoria getting in the way of your seeing the obvious?"

"What?" Owen asked.

"Have you considered Victoria as a possible suspect?"

"No. Why?"

"Does her insurance cover the break-in?"

"I didn't think to ask, Ryan."

"Ask. And open your eyes. Her father had a criminal past."

Owen planted his hands on his hips just above his gun belt. He respected his brother, but Ryan had gone too far. "Don't ever confuse Victoria with her father. I know her father was responsible for Patrick's death, but that was not Victoria's fault."

To his surprise, Ryan smiled. "I guess that answers my question."

"What?"

"You still have feelings for her, and they're interfering with your judgment. Maybe I should put someone else on this case." Ryan's gaze traveled through the room. No one else was in the office, but his eyes rested on Hank Monroe's desk for a couple of meaningful seconds.

Owen found himself chafing at the very idea. Hank had stolen Victoria from him. Hank was still involved with Victoria, somehow. The money in his lunch sack proved that, even if Owen wasn't sure exactly what it meant. "I don't think Monroe is going to be any more objective about Victoria than I would be."

"All right, then answer this one for me—who mailed the Baby Henry package?" Ryan hefted the lightweight box with one hand.

"How would I know?"

"Want to know my theory?"

Owen raised an eyebrow in invitation.

"Whoever mailed this package is trying to send us a

message. They know we've already taken two months to *not* solve Olivia's murder, so they're getting impatient. Not impatient enough to explain everything, but impatient enough to give us a clue. And they wanted to make sure we understood, so they watched until the package was delivered, then showed up in person to fill in all the gaps in the story."

"You think Victoria mailed the package?"

"Open your eyes, Owen." Ryan strode toward the door. "And find out."

Victoria placed the steel wedge atop the hard surface of the log and gave it a couple of taps with the sledgehammer to set it in before taking a step back and giving it a good hard whack.

The wedge went flying.

The log looked completely unscathed.

The knot in her shoulders ached with defeat, but she found where the wedge had landed in the snow, dusted it off and tried again. Thursday morning had arrived with a fresh layer of snow and a gas bill fifty percent higher than any previous since she'd decided to buy the Sugar Plum and return to Fitzgerald Bay.

Was God letting her down?

She'd done her research—looking at all the costs associated with running the inn—and made a thorough investigation before deciding it was the best move for her family. The down payment had required all the money she'd saved from her parents' life insurance policies. The mortgage was only supposed to take up part of her profit, leaving her just enough to live on. Paige would have the small-town upbringing and excellent local schools she deserved. And Victoria would fulfill her mother's dream of owning and operating the very inn her mother had worked for years ago, before cancer had stolen her dreams and her life.

But it wasn't working out that way.

Tapping the wedge in a little harder this time, Victoria stepped back cautiously, raised the sledgehammer and brought it down hard, hoping to send the wedge deep into the wood as she'd seen on the woodsplitting instructional video clips she'd found online.

The wedge went flying into the snow.

"Need a hand?"

"Aaah!" Victoria jumped at the sound of a deep voice behind her, dropping the sledgehammer.

"Sorry to startle you." Owen reached for the sledgehammer and dusted it off, while Victoria took a step back and tried to catch her breath.

"I didn't see you coming. And maybe I am a little jumpy, still. And I'm frustrated with this stupid log." She gave the large piece of wood a kick. "Ow."

"Here, let me see." He picked up the wedge from where it had fallen in the snow. "These things can be tricky." Setting it on the log, he gave it a couple of hard taps—just as she had—and took a step back.

Victoria ducked behind him, hoping to stay out of the path of the flying wedge.

Owen gave the sledgehammer a mighty heave, sinking the wedge deep into the log, splitting it completely in half. The two sides fell wide-open and the wedge clattered to the ground.

"No way." Victoria shook her head. "That's exactly how I did it."

"Maybe you loosened it up for me." Owen reached for the next log, setting the wedge as though about to test his own theory. Victoria watched in disbelief as he split the second log with two hits.

Owen looked over the massive pile of logs that almost filled the small backyard where Victoria and Paige were planning to keep a garden come summer. When she'd delivered decorated birthday cakes for a local farmer's twin granddaughters, she'd spotted their woodpile, and since neither the farmer nor his wife could find their checkbook, she'd bartered the cakes in exchange for the wood—only to learn the wide logs were too big around to fit inside the inn's woodstoves.

"How many of these do you want split?" Owen reached for another log.

"Enough to heat the inn." Victoria sighed as she looked at the pile—which hadn't seemed so big until she'd discovered how difficult the stuff was to split. "The fireplaces in the dining rooms and the suites are high-efficiency woodstoves. I usually keep just enough of a fire going for ambiance, but I thought if I had more wood to burn, I could lower my next gas bill."

"That would do it." Owen split the log cleanly in half with a single swipe before knocking the wood aside, setting on the wedge and splitting another log.

Victoria watched, her emotions swirling. She felt more than a little jealous of his skill, but at the same time grateful for his help, and a bit guilty about letting him do the hard work for her. But he was so much *better* at it than she was.

"I can't let you split all those for me. It's very nice of you, but I'm sure you came by to finish our conversation from yesterday." When he paused in his chopping, she pulled the split wood aside, into a pile closer to the rear door of the inn.

Owen split another log before he answered. "Actually, I had some thoughts on that package Ryan showed us. Normally I wouldn't discuss the details of a case with someone who's not involved with the investigation, but you had a lot of helpful insights, and you knew Olivia. It occurred to me that Olivia might have said something to you—some innocent detail that only looks important when viewed in light of the bigger picture."

"I'd do anything to help."

"I appreciate that." Owen set the wedge in place on another log before looking up at her and explaining quietly, "The lawyer's address listed on the check proved to be a fake. The account has been closed." He slammed the sledgehammer down on the log, giving Victoria the impression that he was frustrated with all the dead ends his investigation had encountered.

He had every right to be frustrated. She felt that way, and she wasn't the one trying to solve the first murder in Fitzgerald Bay in four decades, with the whole town watching.

"What about the lawyer's name? Can't you use that to track him down?"

Owen split a particularly large log with one strike. "He's not listed anywhere—not even a driver's license. The check was probably a scam, anyway. Even if Olivia had wanted to cash it, the thing probably would have been returned unpaid." He emphasized the last word by splitting another log.

Victoria was getting quite a pile of chopped wood out of the conversation, but Owen's words only made her furious. "What kind of low-down dirty slimeball would do such a thing? Taking advantage of Olivia like that, when she's alone and scared and pregnant? When you find the guy, I hope he rots in jail forever."

"*If* we find the guy. But we need whoever mailed that package to step forward and tell us what they know." Owen leaned on the handle of the sledgehammer, and his blue eyes studied her with a troubled intensity.

Between his expression and his words, Victoria got the impression Owen thought she knew something. "Why are you really telling me all this? I thought you said you don't discuss confidential details of people's cases."

"I don't." Owen slammed the sledgehammer down, splitting another log with a chilling crack. He looked back at her. "Not unless I believe there's something important to be gained."

"Are you accusing me of withholding information?" For a moment, Victoria felt indignant. She'd told the police everything she knew about Olivia.

"Have you told me the whole truth?" Owen's piercing gaze stabbed at her heart. "Everything?"

Victoria gulped a shaky breath. No, she hadn't explained to Owen what had happened the weekend of Patrick and her father's death. She'd tried to tell him before, but he hadn't been ready to hear it. She'd tried to respect that. Did he want to know the whole story now? The way he looked at her with eyes that seemed to cut right through to her soul, she couldn't imagine speaking the words out loud.

She *wanted* to tell Owen the truth—to explain the whole story. That was part of why she'd returned to Fitzgerald Bay—part of why she'd brought cookies over to the police station, hoping to catch a moment with Owen and finally purge her guilty conscience. She had to tell him why it had taken her so long to let him meet Paige.

The Bible verse on her fridge said the truth would set her free. Clinging to that promise, she worked up all the courage she could muster. "Owen?"

FIVE

"Yes?" Something that looked like relief filled Owen's expression.

"I need—"

Suddenly the phone in her pocket began to ring. "I need to answer this." She pulled out the phone and checked the caller ID. "It's Paige." Victoria assured her daughter she'd be down to pick her up momentarily. "Don't leave Mrs. Murphy's house. I will be there in three minutes."

"Paige has a cell phone?" Owen asked when she put away her phone.

"For her safety." Victoria watched as sadness filled his eyes. She hadn't meant to remind him of the murderer at large in their community. A cell phone had seemed like a reasonable way to keep tabs on her daughter. "And for my peace of mind. I need to walk down to Mrs. Murphy's. Paige's voice lesson is over."

"I'll accompany you." He leaned the sledgehammer against the inn. "For *your* safety."

"I—" Victoria wanted to protest, to assure him she

didn't feel she was in danger, but those words wouldn't have been entirely true.

"She's my daughter, too."

"I wasn't—"

"Or if you prefer I can stay here and finish splitting your log pile."

"You can come. You have every right to."

Victoria set a brisk pace, not wanting Paige to wait any longer than she already had. Her intention had been to split a few logs in the few spare minutes she had before striking off to fetch Paige. Obviously, Owen's arrival had sent her mind spinning off its track.

The fresh snow and cold weather, chilly even for March in Massachusetts, kept the sidewalks relatively empty of people. Owen sidled up beside her and consulted in a low voice, "I need to know what you know, Victoria."

She tried to work up the courage to speak. Back in high school, they used to talk on the phone for hours. Owen had been closer to her than anyone else. But now ten years stretched between them like a chasm without a bridge.

As she tried to think how to explain all that lay behind them, Owen said, "What do you think about this complication with the lawyer and the bank account being closed? Did Olivia ever talk about needing money?"

"I know Olivia needed money. That's part of why

she took the job as Charles's nanny—that and she was always saying—" Victoria bit back the words as their meaning struck her.

"What?" Owen's steps slowed to match hers.

"She loved children." Victoria shook her head and plodded on.

"That only makes it more curious that she'd let herself become separated from her own child."

"Something criminal was at work," Victoria agreed, glad when Mrs. Murphy's home came into view. Through the row of windows on the sunporch, she could see Paige talking to someone who was just out of sight. At first she thought it might be Mrs. Murphy, but then she recognized the rusty old sedan parked in front of the house. It belonged to Britney, her fresh-out-of-high-school waitress, who she knew aspired to make singing and acting her profession, and who took voice lessons from Mrs. Murphy in the time slot following Paige.

So, Mrs. Murphy and Britney would be busy with the lesson. Then who was Paige talking to?

"I see my father's car." Owen pointed up the street. "He owns Mrs. Murphy's house. She has him over to fix things all the time. Sometimes I wonder if that much needs fixing, or if she's just decided they've both been widowed long enough." Owen gave a chuckle.

Victoria tried to laugh along at the thought of Mrs. Murphy—who had to be a decade older than Owen's father—trying to seduce the chief of police. But at the same time, she felt nervous at the idea of Paige talking to Aiden Fitzgerald—her only living grandfather. Though of course, neither Paige nor Aiden were aware of the fact they were related. It was a reminder of the many discussions that lay ahead.

"Mommy!" Paige squealed happily when Victoria stepped through the front door of the enclosed porch. "I got my first gig!"

"Gig?" Victoria wasn't sure where Paige had picked up the term, but it seemed a tad precocious for her little girl.

Aiden Fitzgerald chuckled. "I arrived just in time to hear this lovely miss singing one of our dear old Irish ballads."

Victoria knew Mrs. Murphy worked on the traditional Irish songs leading up to March, given the town's Irish roots and the annual Saint Patrick's Day celebration. But that didn't explain the *gig*.

"My father loves the songs of the old country," Aiden continued, "but we can't get the young folks interested in them. So when I heard her lovely voice, I knew I had to invite Paige to sing for our family gathering at your café this Saturday."

Victoria felt her mouth open, and she nodded, trying to get a grip on a situation that had been out of her control before she'd even arrived. She was ecstatic to host the Fitzgeralds for Saturday brunch—their reservation during an otherwise not-very-busy hour of the morning was her last hope for being able to make payroll this week. More than that, she saw it as her lone hope for winning the Fitzgeralds' approval. It was a rare opportunity for her to demonstrate that she wasn't just the daughter of the man who'd killed their cousin.

But how could she allow Paige to sing for the Fitzgeralds? What if Owen let leak that she was one of them? Paige had a right to know that information before Owen's extended family, but he and Victoria needed to discuss a lot of details before they were ready to share the whole story with Paige. She was so young and impressionable—she'd want to know everything, including what the future held. And Victoria had no answers to give her.

"I—wow—that's so…" Victoria tried to think of something to say that wouldn't squash the excitement that sparkled in her daughter's eyes. There was nothing she could say, no way to break off her daughter's gig without breaking her heart. "You'll have to practice, Paige. You'll want to know all the words by heart."

"Oh, I will. I will, I will." Paige's blond braids danced as she jumped up and down.

"This is something to look forward to." Owen rubbed his hands together. "I can't wait to hear you sing, Paige."

Owen's words were another reminder that he would

be there Saturday, too. In her café. Watching her daughter—his daughter—sing for his family.

She met his eyes for just a moment, intent on communicating their need to talk, but Aiden spoke first.

"Owen, since you're here, you can give me a hand with the tree branch that broke off in Mrs. Murphy's backyard. This snow was too much for it."

"Sure thing, Dad." Owen looked a little reluctant to let Victoria and Paige leave without him, but he said goodbye and told Paige, "I'll be looking forward to hearing you sing Saturday."

Excited about Aiden's invitation, Paige fluttered like a kite in the wind, tugging on Victoria's arm, fairly pulling her all the way home to the inn up the street. Victoria, like an anchor, hung back, her heart weighed down with heavy thoughts.

They would love Paige. Of course, the whole Fitzgerald family would love her. And then it would happen—the thing she'd feared from the moment she'd learned she was pregnant.

They would take her away.

Victoria had watched in horror ten years before when she'd gone to stay with her aunt and cousin after her father died, and her cousin's friend Natasha had been pregnant. Though Natasha hadn't been a particularly close friend of her cousin, Victoria had immediately felt drawn to her and her story because of their similar situations, both being young, unmarried and pregnant. As she'd watched from a distance, the whole dreadful situation had played out.

Natasha didn't have money or influence or family, but her baby's father did. And her baby's father had wanted custody of the child. At first everyone had insisted it would never happen, but even as Victoria had wrestled with how to tell Owen the truth about the child she carried, Natasha had lost custody of her baby to the wealthy and powerful man who'd fathered him.

Victoria had seen it happen to her cousin's friend and known in the depths of her heart that it could happen to her, too. The Fitzgerald family *owned* Fitzgerald Bay. They were the law, the old money, the very foundation upon which the town was built.

And who was she? The orphaned child of the drunken man whose reckless driving had killed Owen's cousin. They'd take her child just to get even with her. No one in that family had ever cared for her, except Owen, and he would surely want his daughter raised by his family.

The only reason she'd dared to return to Fitzgerald Bay, even now, was because her daughter was finally old enough to choose her—to tell the court or anyone else who might try to take her that she wanted to stay with her mother. But even that hope dimmed in the current circumstances.

She could feel Paige pulling away from her, even as she tugged her arm down the street. She was growing older—rebelling, in her own preteen way. And honestly, who would choose a cash-strapped mom over a father like Owen, anyway? She'd seen them interact. All he'd have to do was open the coffers and Paige would be his.

"Don't you think so, Mom?" Paige tugged on her arm again.

"Think what?" Victoria realized she'd been so lost in thought, she hadn't even caught what Paige was saying.

"My *dress.* The one I wore for Christmas. It will be perfect to wear to sing for the Fitzgeralds. It's emerald-green, like Ireland." Paige twirled around on the sidewalk, clearly imagining how the green dress would flutter around her so prettily.

Victoria smiled a bittersweet smile. Her daughter was beautiful. Who would blame the Fitzgeralds for loving her? "And your green hair bow," she added. "I'll curl your hair."

"Yes!" Paige stopped twirling and jumped up and down again.

As she watched her daughter's smiling face, Victoria couldn't help but wonder if what she felt wasn't a little bit like what Olivia might have felt. Her child had only been a baby, but she'd been taken away from her, whether by death or her father or some other person.

And if the anonymous box delivered to the police station told them anything, someone in Fitzgerald Bay knew more about Olivia's baby than he or she was telling.

* * *

Ryan sat on the edge of Owen's desk and cleared his throat.

Owen looked up from the paperwork he'd been trying to finish. "Yes?"

"Remember Dr. O'Rourke?"

"On the hospital bracelet?"

Ryan nodded. "There are a lot of Dr. O'Rourkes in Ireland, but once we weeded out the psychiatrists and professors, we ended up with just a handful of medical doctors."

"How many deliver babies?"

"Two. One was on vacation the entire week of Baby Girl Henry's birth. The other is Dr. Louise O'Rourke of Dublin. She doesn't recall anything significant about the birth, although her records indicate she delivered a child for one Olivia Henry, age twenty-two."

"So the baby was Olivia's, after all."

"I think we both knew that from the start."

"True." Owen sighed. "But I still hoped maybe the baby belonged to some distant cousin and was being raised by loving parents somewhere—even if it was a long shot."

"Obviously that's not the case. Baby Girl Henry belonged to Olivia."

"The baby lived, then?"

"The doctor believes so."

"Don't the records say—"

Ryan shook his head. "The only record she could

find was the notation in her own personal log. The rest of the hospital records on Baby Girl Henry are missing."

"Misplaced?"

"It doesn't appear so. Less than a week after Baby Girl Henry was born, there was a robbery in the hospital medical records office. At the time, it didn't look like anything had been taken. The lock on the door had been broken, as had the lock on one of the file cabinets, but a cursory search of the files inside didn't turn up anything missing."

Owen rubbed his hands over his face, wishing he could block out the words he feared his brother was about to speak.

"When I asked them to look up records, they realized they should have been in the file cabinet that was broken into. They believe the Henry records were the only ones taken."

"Specifically targeted, then. But why bother? Why was it so important that she couldn't even have hospital records left behind?" Owen puzzled over the new twist in the case.

"They had to have been up to their necks in illegal activity," Ryan assured him. "Breaking and entering to steal evidence isn't something you do unless you're trying to cover up a worse crime."

"So we've got nothing, then. No father, no blood type, no solid evidence other than a blanket and a bracelet and a check that came from nowhere."

Ryan stood. "Someone in town knows more than they're telling. Did you follow up with Victoria?"

"Yes."

"And? What did you learn?"

"She wouldn't tell me anything, but she certainly looked…" He shook his head, still feeling betrayed by what Victoria's response had revealed. He was going to have to question her again, to dig deeper until he learned what she knew. Based on her reaction and the look in her eyes, he was certain she had more to tell him.

"How did she look?" Ryan prompted.

"Like she knows something."

To his credit, Ryan didn't look the least bit happy about Owen's discovery. In fact, his eyes looked sad. "Get to the bottom of it. We need to wrap things up."

Seven-thirty. He had half an hour before the Sugar Plum Café closed. Fortunately, the Friday-evening customers appeared to be clearing out. Maybe Victoria would have a chance to talk to him. Owen wasn't sure he wanted to know the truth—not if it was as ugly as he feared it might be—but Ryan was right. The people of Fitzgerald Bay deserved answers, even if he didn't like what those answers were.

The bell jangled at the door as he stepped in, and Victoria looked up from the computer screen at the hostess's podium with weary eyes.

"Owen." Her greeting was neither smile nor frown.

"Does your father prefer currants or caraway seeds in his Irish soda bread?"

Owen had to smile. The woman never stopped working. "Planning the menu for our family gathering?"

She nodded.

"Dad likes caraway seeds, but I think the rest of us would prefer currants."

"I'll make both, then." She sighed and stepped away from the computer. "Are you here on business, or...?"

"Checking in to make sure everything's okay here." It wasn't the whole truth, but it was still true. "Since your troubles tend to happen around this time of night, I thought I'd make my presence known."

"I appreciate that." For the first time since he'd stepped in, her weary features bore a trace of a smile.

Way to make him feel guilty.

"And I was thinking about our conversation yesterday when we were interrupted by your ringing phone. I don't think you ever had a chance to tell me what you were going to say."

"Oh. Yes." She looked toward the dining room. "Do you mind if I check on Paige a moment? I'll be right back."

"I'll be waiting."

Victoria hurried to Paige's room. Ready as she was to share everything with Owen, she wanted to be certain her daughter wasn't going to walk in on their conversation. That would be the worst possible way for Paige to learn the truth.

Besides that, the mere thought of discussing Paige with Owen made her want to hug her daughter tight, as though she could hold on to her forever.

Paige stretched out on top of the purple comforter that covered her bed and looked up from the book she was reading. "It's not bedtime yet."

"I know, honey. I just—" Her voice caught, in spite of her desire to keep a level head. She sat down beside Paige and tried not to consider the possibility that Owen would take her away. "I just wanted to make sure you're okay." Her voice squeaked up a note.

Paige shoved a bookmark in place and shut her book. "I'm okay, Mom." She looked wary. "Did the bad guy come back?"

"No. No sign of him." When Paige leaned toward her, Victoria scooped her into her arms, planting a kiss on her blond head. "You know I love you, right?"

"You tell me that all the time."

"Do you like living in Fitzgerald Bay?"

"Kind of. Except for the bad-guy part. And I'm ready for summer."

"I'm ready for summer, too," Victoria agreed. "And I wish we didn't have to deal with a bad guy. They're going to catch him soon."

Paige leaned back and looked her mother full in the face. "Is that what you came up here to ask me?

If I like this town? We're not moving again, are we, because you said when we moved here—"

A scream from downstairs filled the house, and both Victoria and Paige jumped to their feet.

"Stay here. Lock your door," Victoria instructed her daughter as she headed downstairs.

"Want me to call the police?" Paige called after her.

"No. They're already here." Victoria practically leaped down the back stairs and landed in the kitchen, where a wild-eyed Charlotte was gasping and pointing.

"A man. He was peeking in the windows. Owen went after him."

Victoria peered through the open doorway in time to see Owen leading a large male figure back toward the inn.

The guy didn't look to be fighting him.

"I just came by to see if Britney was still here," the youth announced as Owen escorted him into the kitchen.

"Britney left already. Did you try calling her?" Victoria looked at the young man and tried to decide if he was big enough to be the shadowy figure they'd seen outside. He was certainly tall, but not as burly as she remembered. But then, a bulky coat might make all the difference.

"I have her phone." The guy pulled away from Owen and, with one hand held up in an innocent gesture, slowly pulled a phone from his pocket with his other hand.

"That looks like Britney's phone." Victoria recognized it. "Do you want me to call her home number?" She looked to Owen for guidance.

He nodded.

Moments later, with Britney on the way, Victoria raced upstairs to assure Paige that everything was all right.

Paige insisted on coming downstairs to see the man who'd been apprehended. As she entered the kitchen, she shook her head. "That's not him."

"Not the same guy who robbed the safe?" Owen clarified.

"He's not as big, and he has an earring." Paige pointed to the young man's ear. "He's not the guy who robbed the safe, and he's not the man from outside the windows, either."

Britney came in the front door a few moments later. "Clint? I thought I told you we were over."

"Fine with me, but I figured you'd want your phone back. You left it in my car."

While the young couple bickered behind her, Victoria steered Paige toward the stairs. "Now it *is* getting close to your bedtime."

Owen cleared his throat behind her.

Victoria felt the muscles in her back tense. Yes, she needed to talk to Owen. Their conversation was ten years overdue. But it wasn't going to be an easy conversation, and she had a frightened child to put to bed first. "Can you come back in half an hour?"

"Thirty minutes." Owen nodded. "I'll be here."

SIX

Owen watched Charlotte lock the door behind her on her way out. He appreciated the hostess letting him wait inside for Victoria to finish getting Paige tucked into bed. Moments later, Victoria descended the stairs.

"I hope you don't mind if I work while we talk." She headed past him for the kitchen. "I still have preparations to make before your family's brunch tomorrow morning."

"Go right ahead. In fact, if there's anything I can do to help…"

"Thanks, but I've got it." Victoria climbed onto a step stool and reached high onto the neatly arranged pantry shelves that edged one wall of the kitchen. She reached above her head and tugged on an enormous sack of flour.

Owen watched the determined woman for a few seconds before he stepped in, planting one foot on the step stool and lifting the fifty-pound sack easily from its perch. He set it on the island countertop behind him and smiled at her.

She looked flustered. "I'm used to doing that myself."

"I thought I could lighten your load." Owen wondered at her independent spirit. Of course she was used to doing everything herself. She'd lost her mother when she was hardly older than Paige, had taken care of her perpetually drunk father and raised Paige by herself for the past nine years.

He watched as she opened the gigantic bag and began measuring out flour into the bowl of an industrial-size mixer near the walk-in fridge doors.

"You wanted to ask me more about Olivia Henry?" She didn't look up as she counted off the cups under her breath.

Never one to beat around the bush, Owen came out and asked the question his brother had sent him to ask. "Did you send the Baby Henry package to the police station?"

Victoria dropped the measuring cup into the mixing bowl and looked as though she'd have tumbled in after it, had the bowl been any bigger. "Of course not!" She retrieved the cup and tapped it on the edge of the bowl to dust it off. "How would I? Why would you even think that?"

"You arrived at the same time as the package. You filled in the gaps in Olivia's story with remarkable insight. Olivia lived here. She was your friend."

"Is that all?"

"You've never brought cookies to the police station before. It seemed suspicious."

Victoria looked at him silently for a moment, her mouth open as though she wanted to speak but wasn't sure where to start. "Let's get one thing straight," she said finally. "The gaps I filled in, in Olivia's story? Those are just theories, okay? I don't *know* anything about Olivia's situation. I was as surprised as anyone that she might have had a baby. That was just me, re-acting to what I saw. Don't think for a second that my version of her story is the way it is. The situation could be completely different. I don't want to point you in the wrong direction."

Owen watched her carefully. Victoria certainly looked as if she was telling the truth, but then, he'd sincerely believed her to be in love with him ten years before. Obviously, based on the way she'd run off with Hank and never looked back, he'd been wrong.

He'd trusted her too much in high school and let his feelings for her cloud his judgment. But every time he looked in her eyes now, he felt the same pull of her allure, the same sympathetic affection that had tricked him into trusting her too much back then. He didn't want to be duped by her again—not when all of Fitzgerald Bay was so eagerly awaiting answers about Olivia Henry's murder.

The measuring cup sat idle in her hands as she stared at it thoughtfully. "How many cups had I measured out?"

"Eight." Owen had paid attention, counting along with her silently in his head.

"Thanks." She started scooping again.

"Next question. What kind of insurance coverage do you have against robbery?"

Victoria stopped scooping flour long enough to explain. "I have small business insurance, but I selected a high deductible and minimum coverage to keep my costs down. Basically, if somebody falls down the steps and breaks a leg, I'm covered. Anything else comes out of my pocket. And if you're suggesting I try to up my coverage at this point, my guess is, after what's been happening around here lately, the price has only gone up."

She scooped two more cups of flour, then dropped the measuring cup again. This time, she didn't bother to pick it up. "Or are you thinking I faked the robbery last week in order to commit insurance fraud?"

Owen shrugged, watching her carefully, hoping for some clear signal that would tell him if she was being honest with him.

Victoria shook her head and looked up at the ceiling. "How can you think that about me? Seriously— like I would try something like that? Like I would frighten my own child by having somebody rob the place?"

"Perhaps Paige was in on it, too." He hated even saying it, but he had to know, to be sure that he could trust her. And he needed to push her to get the truth.

"Right." Victoria nodded. "You think I would ask my own daughter to lie so I could commit a crime?

Paige can sing, so maybe she can act—is that what you're thinking? Honestly, Owen, there was a time when you used to trust me."

The words came out of his mouth before he could stop himself.

"That was before you stole our daughter from me and hid her away for nine years."

Victoria closed her eyes, silently praying for patience and strength. Owen's words made her furious—that he would stand there and patently accuse her like that, and that he would have so little faith in her at all. The man had once said he loved her. But obviously that was a long time ago.

"Owen, what are you really here to learn? Is this about Olivia's case? Or is this about Paige? I offered to tell you the whole story—"

"I don't want to hear about why you ran off with Hank Monroe."

"What?" Victoria had picked up the measuring cup again, but now she pitched it angrily into the bowl of flour, sending up a white cloud. "You think I *ran off* with Hank Monroe?"

"The whole town believes you ran off with him."

Victoria wished she had something else to throw. Instead, she rose up on her tiptoes and got in Owen's face. "Just like back in high school, the whole town believed Hank's stupid story that I slept with him right before our senior year. Is that right? Because everybody knows Hank's dad is a *judge* and my dad was a *drunk,* so Hank must be the one telling the truth, right?"

Owen raised his hands and settled them onto Victoria's shoulders, as though to calm her down.

"Victoria." He whispered her name soothingly near her ear.

"You knew." A little of the fight went out of her as grief and disappointment overcame her anger. "You knew I hadn't slept with *anyone,* Owen." She panted, breathless from fighting him, unsure if she could say what needed to be said. "You knew you were my first, the only man I'd ever been with. You were the only person in the whole town who believed that I hadn't slept with Hank."

Slowly, as her voice went from angry to pleading, Owen's firm grasp on her shoulders relaxed.

Victoria took advantage of the moment to tear herself out of his arms. How could she let him hold her like that, when he didn't even believe her? It would have been far too easy to melt into his arms, to give in to the simmering attraction she felt toward him still. But that would only lead to heartache. She knew no one else in Fitzgerald Bay believed her side of the story—she might have tried to refute the rumor that she'd run off with Hank Monroe if she'd thought anyone would believe her. But Owen's response to the slanderous story was a low blow, and it struck a very tender part of her heart.

She put a few steps' distance between them. "Why did I think you would believe my word over his? Why did I even come back to this stupid town where everyone expects the worst out of me? Obviously I didn't learn my lesson the first time around." She stared at him, wishing he would tell her it wasn't true, that he'd trusted her all along.

Owen said nothing.

Gripping the side of the mixing bowl to steady herself, Victoria picked up the flour scoop and headed back to the bag of flour. She stopped, trying to think.

"Eleven," Owen said softly.

"What?" Distracted by the emotions that raged through her, Victoria wasn't sure where the number came from.

"You have eleven cups of flour in your mixing bowl."

"Thanks." She finished scooping until she had the sixteen cups of flour she needed for her recipe. Then she stopped and looked at Owen, unsure what to do about the man in her kitchen.

"On second thought, maybe I *do* want to hear your side of what happened our senior year."

Victoria let out a long breath, looked at the batch of dough she'd only just started and pinched her eyes shut against all the preparations that still had to be made before brunch, just over twelve hours away.

"But maybe we've said enough for tonight, okay?" he said.

"Okay." The word came out like a sigh of relief.

"Soon, though."

"Soon."

Owen arrived at the Sugar Plum plenty early the next morning for his family's monthly gathering. As he might have predicted, Victoria zipped around the café, waiting on customers, pulling toasty-brown loaves of Irish soda bread from the oven and otherwise looking charming and beautiful as she bustled about her work, her golden hair already escaping from the elaborate twist at her neck.

He watched her silently, still puzzling over her words from the evening before.

Did he believe her? Part of him wanted to, but another part—a large, angry part—was still far too hurt by her betrayal. Whatever she'd done, whether she'd run off with Hank or not, nothing changed the fact that she'd hidden his daughter from him for nine years. She'd purposely, knowingly, cruelly taken away the most valuable gift he'd ever been given, before he'd even known his daughter existed.

So no matter how much he wanted to pull Victoria into his arms and tell her everything would be okay, he wasn't sure he believed it himself. There were still far too many questions that needed answers, but they'd have to wait until after brunch. He'd just have to make himself comfortable and try to enjoy himself.

The first dining room held a roaring fire and a

crowd of Saturday-morning customers settled back into couches or perched on chairs around small tables or in booths. The second dining room, which he'd heard referred to as the front dining room, was a more formal space, also with a fire roaring in the woodstove, but with larger tables and more family-style seating, which at the moment seemed to be occupied by every ladies' society meeting group in town.

Owen headed to the back dining room, a long, slightly narrower room whose pocket doors could be pulled shut for private family gatherings, such as the one his father had reserved it for this morning. Like all the rooms in the café, the walls of the back dining room were filled with photographs of patrons who had visited the place over the years. A wall in the front room held a collection of Massachusetts celebrities, from state politicians to Hollywood movie stars who'd stopped in for lunch while filming in the area. But the back dining hall was mostly local yokels, snapshots of the regular customers who filled the café on a daily basis.

He stood in the open doorway, admiring the photographs.

They dated back for decades. As a child, Owen and his siblings had made a game of finding the people they knew in the pictures. His older brothers always seemed to know more people than he did, but he still felt the challenge stirring within him to see who he could recognize in the pictures on the walls.

There was Pastor Peter Larch from the Fitzgerald Bay Community Church, so long ago his hair didn't even look gray. Another picture showed Burke Hennessy seated at a table with his first wife, Cooper's mother, back when Cooper could barely see over the edge of the table.

He spotted members of Connolly family, his cousins, part of the extended Fitzgerald clan, whose ancestors had founded the town. There was his grandfather, Ian, celebrating his first win as mayor back in 1982. The man had been mayor for longer than Owen had been alive, but he was getting on in years and had announced his plans to retire this year.

As he studied the careworn lines on his grandfather's earnest face, Owen felt the weight of civic duty that had moved his grandfather to take the helm of the town, which had ushered in its most prosperous decades. It was a reminder of the hard work that had built the town, and of all that needed to happen to continue to make Fitzgerald Bay a peaceful place to raise a family.

He needed to catch Olivia's killer. He needed to keep Fitzgerald Bay safe.

The hard clap of heels on the oak floor caught Owen's attention, and he looked up in time to see Christina Hennessy on her way to the ladies' room. "Mrs. Hennessy." He smiled, having just spotted her picture on the wall. "You're looking well today."

Her eyes lit up at his compliment. "I try to stay healthy, but age catches up with us all."

"You don't look any older than you did in this picture." Owen pointed to the photograph on the wall. "How long ago was that taken?"

Christina looked at the picture he'd indicated. "I can't be sure. Excuse me." She continued through to the ladies' room.

Owen blinked, unsure if he'd offended her, and moved on to look at the pictures on another section of wall.

His heart twisted at the sight of a photograph high on the wall. Two beaming boys looked straight into the camera, their arms slung around each other's shoulders, chocolate-milk moustaches dripping from their upper lips.

Himself. And Patrick.

His cousin, his closest family member by age, practically his best friend for seventeen years. Though they'd drifted apart somewhat in high school, back when they were growing up, he and his cousin had been almost inseparable. He still missed their conversations sometimes, and the innocent games they'd play.

He swallowed hard against the lump in his throat. Patrick's death had changed everything. In some ways, Owen wondered if maybe he still wasn't over it. Like the great divide, it separated the innocence of his youth from the jaded reality of adulthood.

Patrick had simply been out for a drive. Victoria's father had crossed the centerline, hitting Patrick's car head-on, killing them both.

At the time, Owen had been dating Victoria. Or at least, he thought he had been. He'd gone to bed one night content in the knowledge that his cousin was his best friend and Victoria loved him. He'd awakened the next morning to learn that his cousin was dead, and Victoria's father was, too.

His first thought had been to find Victoria. When her mother had died, back when they were both in the fourth grade, he remembered her sitting at her desk, weeks and even months later, with tears running silently down her cheeks. He'd wanted to comfort her, but at ten years old, he hadn't known how. So when he found out her father had died, his first instinct had been to pull her into his arms and hold her while they both cried.

Except that she was gone. He called her house, he went to her house, he called all their friends. No one knew where she'd gone.

Hank Monroe had left town the same day. When Owen had first heard the rumor that they'd run off together, he'd refused to believe it. Victoria had gone out with Hank only once before she and Owen had begun dating their senior year of high school. She'd adamantly insisted that she couldn't stand Hank, that he was pushy and after only one thing.

Her insistence hadn't quieted the rumors, then or

now. Then, Hank had claimed they'd slept together. Victoria had denied it all through their senior year, and Owen had believed her, even defended her, though he knew he couldn't change what people believed.

Ten years later, Owen still wondered if he'd been naive to accept her word, or if, as some suggested, she'd simply been playing him, using him to make Hank jealous so she could get back together with him.

"Hi!" A cheerful voice greeted him from the doorway, tearing his thoughts from the past. Emerald-green satin twirled in a circle, and when Paige came to a stop facing him, her smile was bright.

And familiar.

Owen looked back at the picture of him and Patrick.

He looked back to Paige.

Eerie.

She had her mother's delicate arched eyebrows instead of his stockier, straighter brows. Her long blond hair was curled into ringlets and tied with a bow. But besides those minor details, she looked just like the picture of him at the same age. He blinked and looked back and forth between the two again.

Paige didn't look much like Patrick, or any of the other young folks on the walls. She looked *like him*.

The little girl danced with impatience. "What do you think of my dress? Is it okay?"

Owen found his voice at last. "Okay? It's so beautiful I can hardly find words to describe it."

Paige giggled with delight and pranced closer. "Are you excited to hear me sing?"

"I got here early so I could get a good seat. Where do you think I should sit?"

Beaming, Paige surveyed the room and took her time analyzing his seating options, suggesting several different places where he might have a good view.

Owen tried to keep up with her words, but he couldn't help watching Paige and wondering if anyone else could see what he saw so clearly. Cooper Hennessy had already guessed it. What if someone else realized the truth, and let on to Paige before he had a chance to get to know her and tell her himself?

"Paige?" Victoria hurried into the room. "There you are. Help me in the kitchen, will you, honey?"

Paige smiled. "Sure, Mom."

He looked at Victoria. "I look forward to talking to you at some point." He turned to Paige. "And I can't wait to hear you sing, Paige."

Paige beamed and headed toward the kitchen.

"Yes," Victoria said, her back already to him as she followed Paige. "When I have a spare moment."

Owen couldn't imagine when Victoria would have a spare moment, not with the busy morning they had planned. But he was getting impatient. He'd talked to Cooper again about the possibility of joint custody, and he was going to need a lot of answers in order to make his case.

And he *would* make his case. As he looked back

and forth between the picture on the wall and his daughter sparkling in her green dress, he became only that much more certain. Paige was his daughter, and it was only right that he finally share custody of his child.

Victoria could feel Owen's eyes on her every time she entered the room. Yes, he wanted answers. She wanted answers, too. But in the meantime, his family members wanted coffee and rolls and corned beef and cabbage. Food was more urgent than questions.

Bless her heart, Paige was helping out, toting napkins and jelly and cookies and spoons. But Victoria stopped short of letting her carry hot beverages. "We can't risk spilling on your dress," she reminded her daughter.

Once everyone had been served and the fervor had more or less died down, Aiden Fitzgerald, Owen's father, tapped his spoon against his water glass, and the Fitzgerald clan fell silent as he announced their entertainment.

Victoria nervously seated herself at the piano. Mrs. Murphy wasn't able to be there to accompany Paige, so Victoria had dusted off her piano-playing skills enough to hammer out the tune. She and Paige had been practicing every spare minute on the dining room piano—much to the amusement of customers who'd happened by and caught them at it. As long as neither of them was overcome by nerves, they just might make it through the song.

"'Be Thou my vision, oh Lord of my heart,'" Paige began in her sweet little voice, the words almost lost amidst the haunting melody. But as she got caught up in singing the old Irish hymn, her voice grew stronger. When Paige reached the line, "Thou my great Father, I Thy true son," Victoria's fingers faltered on the keys, but she quickly recovered, and Paige didn't seem to notice, and no one else did, either. It wasn't until Paige finished the last lingering line that Victoria looked up and caught Owen looking at her.

What was he thinking? His features were hardened, void of any emotion except maybe simmering anger.

The entire family clapped enthusiastically, and Victoria ducked out of the room, pausing just long enough to make sure Paige wasn't overwhelmed. From the looks of it, she was enjoying herself immensely.

Owen watched Victoria exit. Much as he would have liked to go after her and demand answers to his questions, he couldn't move. His heart was hammering far too hard inside him.

Victoria had blushed when Paige had reached the line about the father and his son. What if someone guessed why she'd faltered? He tried to tell himself there was nothing behind it—the song was about being a child of God. God was the father in question, not any human.

But the way his own throat had tightened hearing his daughter sing those words, he knew exactly why Victoria had stumbled. It was a reminder he desperately needed. Though he wasn't sure he was ready for Paige to learn the truth, he'd rather she hear it from him than wait for rumors to start circulating.

Paige soon scampered off after her mother, and Owen hoped the gathering would end before long. But another spoon tinkled against another water glass, and this time, Owen's older brother Douglas stood and cleared his throat.

"As many of you know, I've been seeing Merry here for a while." Douglas looked as if he was fidgeting with something in his pocket, and Owen wondered what was up. He was used to his brother being strong and witty, and a reasonably talented public speaker. Now Douglas looked as though he might pass out at any moment.

"I've never met a woman who—" Douglas cleared his throat and looked up, and seemed to be struggling to speak.

Were his eyes moist?

Owen was concerned. Was his brother having a heart attack? He was only thirty-four, but what other explanation was there for the bizarre symptoms Douglas appeared to be exhibiting? His face had grown pale, and his lower lip even seemed to be trembling.

Suddenly, Douglas dropped down, almost out of

sight behind the crowd of Fitzgeralds surrounding the table.

Owen pulled out his phone. He'd give his brother another thirty seconds to pull himself together, and then he was going to call for an ambulance.

"Merry, my love—" Douglas took Meredith O'Leary's hand "—would you do me the honor of being my bride?"

The room went completely silent. Even the patrons in the next dining room grew silent. Owen put his phone away.

"Yes!" Merry practically threw herself at Douglas, kissing him, while the room erupted into cheers, and the folks the next dining room over who'd been listening in started clapping.

Victoria even peeked her head around, with Paige at her heels, to check on the commotion. Owen watched as Victoria realized what was happening, saw her smile a wistful-looking smile and lean down to whisper something to Paige, who quickly started clapping, too.

Then Victoria glanced his way, and her blush returned, and she darted back in the direction of the kitchen.

Owen watched her go. Mystifying woman. She looked sincerely happy for Douglas and Merry. And she was obviously a good mother to Paige. But what about the rest of this mess, with what she might be hiding about Olivia's secret baby, and of course, the secret she'd kept from him for nine years?

Turning back to the happy couple, Owen watched Douglas receive instructions on the claddagh ring he'd bought for Merry, about which finger it should be worn on, and which way it should point, and all the complicated meaning behind it. None of that romantic nonsense was Owen's kind of thing to sort out, but at the same time, he couldn't help feeling a bit like that wistful smile he'd glimpsed on Victoria's face.

Douglas, at least, was going to have a family. Merry had a four-year-old son, and if Douglas took after the family tradition at all, they'd have a houseful of kids in a few short years. He felt a pang of jealousy that Douglas was going to have a family.

Owen looked around the table at his siblings. It was high time their large brood of single folks did something to secure another generation. If it had been up to Owen, he'd have gotten married years ago and have a bustling family filling this table by now.

But it hadn't been up to Owen. The only girl he'd ever loved had run away ten years before, leaving Owen feeling too jilted and hurt to bother looking for someone else to love. But he had a daughter, an adorable, talented, nine-year-old daughter who looked just as he had at that age. It was time for him to start being the father he should have been all along.

As he looked over in time to see his brother and Merry sharing a loving kiss, Owen realized it was time. The future wouldn't wait forever. Cooper had advised him that joint custody of Paige might not even be possible, and had suggested that Owen work out an agreement with Victoria first, rather than starting with a legal filing.

But based on the interactions he'd observed between Victoria and her daughter, he couldn't imagine her being willing to share custody. Paige had been hers alone for nine years.

But she was *his* daughter, too. Victoria would have to accept that and everything it meant, or maybe he would have to talk to Cooper Hennessy about petitioning for joint custody, after all.

SEVEN

"Victoria?" Owen's deep voice came out of nowhere just as Victoria slumped into a booth with a tall glass of chocolate milk and the last wedge of Irish soda bread.

Victoria jumped to her feet. "When did you come back?"

"I never left." He motioned with his hand for her to sit. "We need to talk."

Victoria settled back into her seat, but she couldn't relax. She washed down a bite of bread, hoping to calm her stomach. But the agitation she felt inside had nothing to do with hunger.

"Paige went with my father to the Reading Nook. He gave her a gift certificate to my sister's bookstore in exchange for singing for us," Owen relayed.

"I know. Your father didn't have to do that, but Paige was thrilled. She loves to read." Victoria took another bite of bread.

"We need to tell Paige that I'm her father."

Though Owen's words seemed to come out of

nowhere, in many ways, Victoria had been expecting them for some time.

"I agree." She set her bread down calmly and met his eyes. "Especially after seeing the two of you interact today, it's only a matter of time before someone guesses, and I don't want her to learn the truth through the grapevine. But the first thing she's going to want to know will be what kind of role you'll have in her life. She's talked before about having a father—"

"She has? When? What has she said? What did you tell her?"

Victoria felt her heart thumping hard, and she pushed away the napkin that held her bread, unable to think about eating when Owen looked at her with such intensity in his blue eyes, the crisp cut of his brown hair giving him a militant look that made him only that much more intimidating. "For years she's noticed other kids with their mothers and fathers, and asked about families. Of course, we've always known other single moms, so I explained that our family was one of those families, not the kind with two parents."

Anger flashed in Owen's eyes. "But she *has* two parents."

"Not functionally."

"I would have functioned—"

Victoria reached across the table and took Owen's hand as his volume began to rise. They were alone in the café, but anyone could walk in at any moment. "You *can* function as her father, if you want to. But we need to agree on what your role will be before Paige asks that question."

To her surprise, Owen fell silent, though the fury in his eyes didn't dim.

"Owen," Victoria asked gently, "what do you want?"

"I want my daughter in my life."

"Okay. How do you want us to divide her time?"

"You got the first half of her childhood. I just want to make sure I have an equal share in the rest. I want to share in her parenting, Victoria. I want my parental rights."

His words, combined with the serious look on his face, sent a chill down Victoria's spine. She dropped his hand. "You want—"

"I want joint custody. I want her to come live with me for half the week."

Victoria stared at him.

"But she hardly knows you."

"Because you never gave her a chance to get to know me. You created this situation, Victoria." The anger she'd seen simmering in his eyes spilled over, and he rose up onto his feet.

Victoria jumped from her seat, too, glad there wasn't anyone around to witness their heated exchange. "You can't take her away from me. She'll be terrified."

"Terrified of her own father? And I'm not taking her *away,* Victoria." Owen glared at her and strode for the door, as though he was going to find Paige and take her home that very instant.

"Wait! Where are you going?"

"To find Cooper Hennessy."

"Why—" Victoria started to ask, but quickly understood. "You're going to take me to court?"

"If that's the only way for me to attain shared custody, yes." He stepped past her toward the door.

"Owen, wait." She tugged on his arm. Shared custody might be just the *beginning.* She couldn't begin to afford a court battle, especially not against the wealthy, influential Fitzgeralds. Owen *had* to be convinced otherwise. "Stop and think. Calm down. You can't do this to Paige. It would tear her apart. Please be reasonable. We can work something out." She gently pushed him back toward the kitchen, away from the front windows where anyone passing by on the street might see them.

His chest rose and fell with barely suppressed emotion under her hands. "You've had her for over nine years."

"I'm sorry. I can't change the past. I wish I could go back in time and change the way everything happened, but I can't. The best we can do is to make the right decisions from here on out. Please?"

"I want my daughter in my life. She's a Fitzgerald. She ought to be raised as a Fitzgerald." He didn't specify what that meant, but Victoria imagined it came with a lot more privileges than being raised as an Evans.

Victoria nodded. "I'm willing to share parental rights with you." Her voice broke, and she felt tears streaming down her cheeks. "But you've got to let her get to know you first. You can't just take her away half the week or she'll be traumatized. She has to trust you. She has to understand that we both love her and we want what's best for her."

"She's my daughter. She should be a Fitzgerald. She should have the name."

"Okay. We can change her name. But we can't move any faster than what she's comfortable with." Victoria sniffed back her tears. "Okay?"

For the first time, Owen's stony expression softened ever so slightly. "Okay."

Owen stepped out onto the street and took a deep breath of the crisp March air. He'd gotten what he'd asked for, more or less. It was a victory.

He headed up the street. The Hennessy Law Office was closed for the weekend, but first thing Monday morning he was going to have Cooper draw up papers, and then make sure Victoria signed them before she changed her mind. Maybe then, once all the legal details were taken care of and there was no chance of going back, maybe he'd finally feel at peace about the situation. Once he had parental rights, no one could take his daughter away from him.

He made it about another block, almost halfway home, before guilt struck him.

Picking up his pace, he broke into a trot, almost as though he could outrun the remorse that seemed to have grabbed him by the ankle, creeping up his body like some parasitic weed.

It was silly. There was no reason for him to feel guilty. Paige was his daughter and he had every right to share in her life. Even Victoria had said so.

By the time he reached his town house a few blocks from town, he was out of breath—which was absurd, because he often ran far longer distances without getting winded. He pulled out his keys and pinched his eyes shut, hoping to block out thoughts of Victoria, but all he could see in his mind's eye was her tear-filled face as she pleaded with him not to take her daughter away.

The clinging vine of guilt held his arms back, preventing him from so much as unlocking the door, so Owen leaned against the doorway, panting as he fought it.

Victoria had taken Paige away from him. She'd wronged him. She deserved every tear she'd shed.

And yet, how many times back in high school had he held her while she cried over the loss of her mother and her struggles to keep her dad sober, or at least off the road when he'd been drinking? How many times had he prayed that somehow, he could make all those tears go away for good?

That had pretty much been the last time he'd prayed, save for the peace of his own mother's soul when she died of cancer five years ago. With Patrick dead and Victoria gone, Owen had felt as though the light of his faith had been snuffed out.

Now he pulled it out like a rusty weapon and held it up toward the light.

"God?" he whispered into the cold March air, the prayer almost creaking for lack of use. "I don't know if I did the right thing."

He waited, watching the white puffs of his panting breath give way to normal breathing. He could almost feel the choking vine of guilt halt its steady climb. "I don't know what I'm supposed to do. Paige is my daughter. I deserve—" He stopped, the pressure on his heart growing again.

Did he deserve her?

He looked up, as though he could see God through the misty Massachusetts sky.

"I don't know what I'm supposed to do," he repeated, and shook his head, weary from the emotional fight. "I don't know." He shook his head again. Was God even listening?

Of course not. What was he thinking, letting guilt get the better of him?

Shrugging off the assault of emotions, he went in and closed the door behind him. Rousing his laptop from sleep mode, he pulled up Cooper's email address from his local contacts and started typing.

Adding on the agreement he and Victoria had reached, Owen made his case to Cooper. He knew enough about the law to know it was a solid case. Victoria had agreed to give him shared custody of Paige, and even if she went back on her word, surely he had rights?

He finished the email and hit Send.

His daughter would be his, one way or another.

Victoria spent every spare moment with Paige the next day, as though she could store away precious memories against the time when Owen would take her daughter away from her for hours, nights at a time. They spent Sunday morning at church together, and Paige giggled as she helped decorate cookies most of the afternoon. After the supper crowd cleared out, Victoria hurried upstairs to get in some reading time with Paige before bed.

It was just after eight-thirty on Sunday evening when Victoria and Paige sat reading in the big comfy chair in Paige's room, and Victoria heard a sudden thump from somewhere below them.

One glance at her daughter's face told her Paige had heard the sound, too.

"What was that?" Paige whispered.

"Shh." Victoria listened intently, straining to hear the sound if it came again, while at the same time praying it was nothing. They'd been jumping at every odd creak and groan in the old house since the robbery the week before. But just to be on the safe side, Victoria pulled out her phone.

A clatter like breaking glass erupted from downstairs, and Paige leaped from her lap, pushing her bedroom door shut and locking the simple hook-and-eye mechanism, while Victoria called 911, quickly relaying the situation.

"I think they're in the back dining room," she explained. "The front door is locked, but you could send an officer around the side." Part of her shuddered at the thought of her antique wood-inlaid door being kicked in. That would cost several thousand dollars to replace. But then, there was no price she could put on Paige's safety. Ultimately, she just wanted whoever was downstairs to be caught.

"An officer is on the way. Would you like to stay on the line?"

"Yes, please."

Paige snuggled into her arms, and Victoria tucked her daughter's head under her chin, praying for their safety, praying that the nightmare they were living through would soon come to an end.

The instant Owen heard the call come over the radio, he whipped his cruiser around in a one-eighty and floored it the three blocks between him and the Sugar Plum, throwing the vehicle into Park and leaping out a quarter of a block from the inn, hoping to avoid scaring off whoever might be breaking in.

The dispatcher had relayed a report of breaking glass in the back dining room. Owen had spent most of the previous day in that room and knew it well. He drew his sidearm and darted up the sidewalk toward the wide windows that flanked the side of the building.

There were no lights on downstairs, but Owen caught sight of movement—a curtain fluttering through the open window.

Make that the *broken* window.

At the same time, a figure at the front door caught his attention. Owen hesitated, unsure which direction to go. Was the perpetrator retreating through the front door?

Ducking behind a front tree, Owen focused on the front door as it opened and the figure stepped through.

Light filled the foyer.

Owen heard a thump from the side of the building. He zipped back, trying to cover both sides of the building at once. A dark figure darted behind the building. Owen gave chase, vaulting the woodpile and nearly stumbling as he tried to keep his footing on the uneven terrain.

The figure passed under the glow of a streetlight, and for a moment, Owen had a decent glimpse of the perpetrator from the back. Not tall, not a big guy like the robber Paige had described. No, this intruder was slightly built, even feminine, with a flutter of blond hair escaping from beneath a dark hat.

Owen sprinted toward the moving figure, who disappeared past the next building. But as Owen rounded the corner, a vehicle tore off with a squeal of tires, leaving nothing but sloppy snow in its wake. Thick snow obscured the small sedan, leaving him with no make, model or license plate number. Even the hubcaps were little more than a generic blur.

Mindful of the figure he'd spotted at the front door, Owen gave up trying to run down the speeding car on foot and swiftly rounded the front of the building, leaping up the front steps and through the open door just as a familiar plump figure backed her way out from behind the hostess podium.

"Aaah!" Charlotte Newbright screamed and dropped whatever she was carrying with a loud thud.

Owen looked down at what she'd dropped.

Shoes.

Shoes weren't very incriminating.

He threw on the lights to the next dining room and passed through to the back hall, where a cold draft from the broken window had blown the curtains in and out, snagging the rich fabric on the jagged edges of the glass.

Another expense Victoria didn't need—a new window and new curtains, too. Add to that the horrible mess that covered the floor: pictures torn from the walls, their glass shattered, their frames askew. Owen shoved his sidearm back into its holster and got on his radio, informing the dispatcher across the street that she could let Victoria know it was safe to come downstairs.

He tromped back through to the foyer, where Charlotte had picked up her shoes and was glaring at him with a red face.

"Just what is the meaning of this?" She gestured at him with one sodden sneaker. "Scaring me half out of my wits?"

"Did you catch someone?" Victoria peeked around the corner of the stairwell. "Charlotte!"

"Charlotte?" Paige echoed, descending the stairs.

"Wait, Paige." Victoria placed one hand on Paige's shoulder, holding her back. She looked at Owen. "Is it safe?"

Owen scanned the rear dining room and Charlotte before he answered Victoria. "It's safe to come down, but don't go in the rear dining room. Not yet." He turned his attention back to the hostess. "What are you doing here?"

Her face almost as red as her hair, Charlotte held up her shoes. "I came to get my snow boots." She stomped with one booted foot. "It's snowing. We're supposed to get six inches overnight, and I knew I'd need my boots to come to work in the morning."

"So you came out in the snow to get your boots, and got your shoes covered with snow, so that you wouldn't have to get your shoes covered with snow in the morning?"

"Yes." Charlotte nodded as though the explanation made perfect sense.

Owen raked a hand back through his hair, frustrated by the fallout of her untimely arrival.

"I'm confused." Victoria reached the bottom of the stairs, one protective arm still wrapped around Paige's shoulders. "If Charlotte came in through the front door for her boots, why did we hear breaking glass below Paige's room, in the rear dining room?"

"Someone broke in through the dining room window. That was the sound of breaking glass you heard."

"Where are they now?"

"When Charlotte flipped on the front lights, the intruder escaped around the back of the house. I tried to give chase, but the perpetrator had a head start and a vehicle waiting."

Paige looked up at him with wide eyes. "They got away?"

"Yes." The disappointed look on his daughter's face made him feel that much more defeated.

"Did you get a good look at him? Was it the same bad guy I saw?"

Owen took a deep breath before responding. He felt hesitant to share too much of what he'd learned in front of Charlotte. Whether he liked it or not, her proximity to the recent break-ins was too suspicious. "Actually, Paige, there are some things I need to take care of before we can talk about this." He turned to Charlotte. "You can head home now, if you'd like."

"Thank you. I've got an early morning tomorrow, and it's getting late." She took her shoes and headed out the door.

Owen turned to Paige and Victoria. "And I suppose it's getting late for you, too. Don't you have school tomorrow?"

"She does. I'll tuck her in and then I need to see the damage." Victoria pointed their daughter back up the stairs, and her slender figure disappeared around the bend in the stairway.

Owen took his time looking at the footprints in the backyard. The fleeing intruder had left several deep impressions, though the falling snow was quickly obscuring them. Still, he was able to get measurements and pictures before they disappeared entirely.

Investigating the mess inside proved to be more complicated. Broken glass littered most of the floor. Owen knew the mess would have to be cleaned up before Victoria could allow customers anywhere near the room. But at the same time, he wanted to take his time picking through the pieces in hopes of finding something that might help identify the perpetrator. He also needed to figure out a way to secure the broken window against the cold night air, which wasn't going to help Victoria's gas bills any.

The rotten feeling that had claimed him since his conversation with Victoria the day before now felt even worse. The perp had gotten away. His daughter wasn't safe. He was failing at everything.

He heard Victoria's soft footfalls approaching, and her gasp told him she'd seen the mess.

Owen didn't look up from the glass fragments he sifted through. "Do you have anything we can nail over the window to secure it for now?"

"I think there are some boards in the basement." She sounded a little breathless. "I can look."

"Do you need a hand?" He glanced back over his shoulder, but Victoria had already left the room.

A few minutes later she was back with boards, nails and a hammer. "This isn't going to be pretty."

Owen helped her juggle the materials. "Maybe I should pound them on from the outside. That will save your woodwork, and we won't have to step across the broken glass."

"Okay." Victoria's voice trembled, and she pinched her full lips together as though struggling not to cry.

That was the last thing he needed. He still hadn't sorted out what to do about the guilt he felt for making her cry the day before, but it didn't make any sense to revisit the deal he'd fought so hard for. Paige was supposed to be his—he just wished Victoria wouldn't cry about it. If she started tearing up again, he didn't know what he'd do.

He tried to get her mind off the mess. "Did Paige go to bed okay?"

"Yeah. I locked our apartment door. She has her

cell phone under her pillow. I don't think she really understands what happened—just that she got to stay up past her bedtime. I'm more spooked than she was." Victoria looked up at him. Though her words sounded as if she was trying to be lighthearted, he could see real fear behind her brown eyes.

"Let me go out and put these boards up. I'll be right back. Don't clean up this mess just yet, but I would appreciate it if you could look over the pictures and see if you can tell if anything is missing."

"Sure thing."

Owen trudged outside and managed to secure the boards with a fairly tight fit to the window frame. It wasn't the most energy-efficient patch job, but it would keep the snow out.

When he came back in, Victoria held a framed picture in her trembling hands. The glass was cracked, but it didn't appear that the photograph inside had been damaged.

Owen looked at the smiling woman in the picture and felt his heart give a dip. "Your mother?"

Victoria nodded. "She was the head pastry chef here for eight years, until her cancer made her too weak to work."

"We were in the fourth grade." His words came out as a whisper. He didn't need to be reminded of how much sympathetic pain he'd felt when Victoria had suffered that loss. He'd never known anyone who'd lost someone they loved so much. He couldn't fathom the kind of pain she must have felt. In many ways, he realized he still didn't understand it. His own mother had been much older when she'd died, and though he'd loved her, she hadn't been the center of his universe as Victoria's mother had been to her.

"Paige will be in the fourth grade next year." Victoria set the picture reverently on a table. "I think of all the things my mother taught me—about baking, about life—and it makes me wonder—" Her voice caught, and she looked up at the ceiling as though she could see straight through to where her little girl slept.

Owen looked up, as well. He knew what Victoria needed to hear, but if he admitted it to her, could she use it against him to make a case for keeping her daughter?

He watched a tear trickle down her cheek.

Mush—that's what he turned to every time those brown eyes cried. He'd been angry enough the day before to resist the tug of her tears, but he'd felt so bad ever since that it didn't take more than one tear this time.

"You're doing a great job with Paige."

"Right. With our home being broken into, and Paige almost walking in on a robbery in progress—and who knows how I'm going to make this month's mortgage payment and pay for this." She pointed to the broken windows, and the curtains that had been shredded by the broken glass, which hung limp now that the wind had been blocked.

Owen took a tentative step closer. "It's going to be okay."

"Sure." Victoria nodded. "Just like it was okay when my mom got sick? It was her dream to buy this place. She actually had made plans—she had a savings account built up and everything. But then she ended up spending it all on medical bills. I thought I could make her dream come true, but look at the mess I'm making." Her gaze fell to the broken glass littered across the floor.

"You didn't make this mess."

"No, I didn't. But I'm the one who's got to clean it up." She looked at him with red-rimmed eyes. Her strained voice dropped to a whisper. "What is God doing?"

The faltering hitch in her voice made Owen catch his breath. Reaching for her, he slid one arm across her shoulders, surprised when she didn't fight him but instead settled her cheek against his shoulder. His first thought was the somewhat shocking realization that Victoria still wore the same perfume she'd worn in high school—the same enthralling scent that had so beguiled him when they'd first dated.

"God will see you through," he assured her automatically, though his words felt like hollow platitudes. What did he know about overcoming adversity? When Patrick had died and Victoria left him, he'd pretty much stuck his head in the sand. In a lot of ways, it was still there.

Wrapping his arms a little more securely around her, Owen felt himself drawn back in time to the days when he'd held Victoria and dreamed they'd be together forever. She'd felt just right in his arms then. In spite of all that had come between them, he still found himself wanting to hold her close to his heart.

It was strange, because he knew she didn't belong there. This was the woman who'd kept his daughter a secret from him.

So why couldn't he resist her? Was it because he was weak, or just foolish? Obviously he still hadn't learned his lesson when it came to letting Victoria get close to him.

She sniffed back her tears and looked at the mess on the floor. "Is it okay if I start sweeping, or do you still need to investigate?" She didn't question his reassuring words. Probably because he hadn't managed to make them sound very reassuring.

"I took pictures of the crime scene." Owen stepped back, releasing her, chastising himself for instantly wishing she was still in his arms. "Let me help you."

"I'm sure you've got to get back to work."

"They'll call me if they need me. Who knows, we might find an important clue." He wasn't about to leave her. Not now, not like this, with her dining room—and her faith—in shambles.

EIGHT

Victoria tried to focus on sweeping up every last shard of glass, instead of letting herself dwell on the nastiness of what had happened. She wished she could sweep away her problems as easily as clearing away the glass that littered the floor.

Besides being forced to work alongside the man who was planning to take her daughter away, there was the ongoing onslaught on her business. So many irreplaceable pictures had been ruined. She prayed they wouldn't be damaged beyond repair. And in the background of all those material questions, she couldn't seem to sort out the *why* behind it all.

"What do you think was the motive here, anyway?" she asked Owen as he tossed shards of broken glass into a wastebasket.

"It's hard to say. Considering that your last break-in was on a Sunday night, too, maybe the same party thought they could get another hefty take. Has your new safe arrived?"

"Not yet."

"So they might have been looking for another safe in the wall. This wall has a large empty space behind it."

"The chimney runs behind there."

"That explains the space. If a thief didn't know about the chimney, it stands to reason they might look for a safe behind the pictures. Whatever they were looking for, I don't think they had time to find it."

Victoria agreed. "I was too busy to get the deposit made on Saturday, as usual, but I took the money up to the church. Pastor Peter arranged for me to put it in the church safe—the same safe where they keep the Sunday offering."

"How many people know it's there?" Owen asked.

"Just me and the pastor, and the treasurers who oversee the safe."

"Charlotte doesn't know?"

Victoria froze, then slowly started sweeping again. "No, she doesn't. That doesn't help her story, does it?"

"I don't like to think she would be involved in this, but I would have caught the intruder if she hadn't turned on the lights when she did."

"So what do you think, then?"

"She might have been working with a team, waiting to give the signal if they needed to retreat."

"A *team?*"

"Assuming we're dealing with the same party that robbed you last week, yes, there would have to be at least two people involved. Last week the robber was a man. This week it was definitely a small-framed woman. Both the visual I got on the retreating perp and the footprints I found outside prove that."

Victoria leaned back and took a deep breath. "So, you think this is some kind of organized assault against me? There haven't been any other targets in town?"

"As far as I know, you're the only one who's experienced this kind of activity."

She wanted to remain strong, for her own sake and for her daughter, but Victoria couldn't shake the feeling of terror that began to choke her as Owen spoke. "So they're coordinated?"

"Yes."

"And they're determined?"

"It would seem so."

A whimper of fear escaped from her lips. "What are they going to do next?"

Owen couldn't take it any longer. Yes, he still felt bitter toward Victoria for hiding Paige from him, but the woman was folding under the pressure. Whatever lies she may have told him in the past, he couldn't stand back and watch her suffer—not when he knew his own inability to catch her intruders had complicated the situation for her. It didn't feel right to keep his distance from her when she was hurting. It felt right only when she was in his arms.

He wiped the dust from his hands and took a step

closer to the trembling woman. "I'm sorry this has happened to you."

"I just don't understand. Who did this? And why? Does it have something to do with Olivia's murder? With the secret baby?" She sniffled.

Owen picked up a napkin from a nearby table and handed it to her, moving closer in case she decided she needed to cry on his shoulder again.

"Thanks." She wiped at her tears but didn't move any closer to him. Obviously she was wary of the feelings between them, too. "When Detective Delfino was staying here, he asked to have Olivia's room. Then it was ransacked. I know you guys concluded that the guy from Boston was behind that, but what if there's something in this house? What if— Wait."

Victoria looked at the pictures and blinked, her eyebrows scrunched up with thought. "You asked if Olivia ever gave me anything. Well, she did." She crossed the room to another wall and plucked down a picture that was hanging in the corner. "I had forgotten all about this."

"What is it?" Owen stood close to Victoria as they both peered at the picture. There was the scent of her perfume again, tempting him to pull her close. It took him a few seconds to focus his thoughts.

"Olivia wanted me to hang this picture on the wall. She said she wanted to feel like she was a part of this town. At the time I thought it was a strange request, but I didn't see any harm in it."

The picture showed two smiling figures standing on a cliff side overlooking the sea. "This shoreline isn't near here, is it?"

"No. This was taken in Ireland—I guess about twenty-three years ago."

"Who's the man in the picture? He looks familiar, but I can't place him." Owen studied the smiling face that seemed to taunt him with its anonymity. Shaggy dark hair hung to his eyes, but Owen was sure he recognized the man's jovial smile. But from where?

Victoria tapped on the glass. "Olivia said this is a picture of her parents, before she was born. This man is Olivia's father. Her mother died a couple of years ago."

"What happened to her dad? I feel like I've seen him before."

"She said she had no contact with him when she was growing up. In fact, she made a big deal about never having known him, about missing growing up with a father figure in her life. She stirred up Paige to want to find out who her father is."

"Has Paige asked about me?"

There was that guilty look back in Victoria's eyes. "Yes."

Owen thought about pushing further, demanding Victoria allow him to tell Paige sooner, but choking guilt grabbed him quickly. He'd told Victoria he'd ease into getting to know his daughter first.

Besides, he was on duty. He was supposed to be

investigating the robbery and Olivia's murder. "Did Olivia ever mention her father's name? Does he live in Ireland?" Owen looked at the man in the picture, the smile that seemed to mock him with its namelessness. "I feel like I've seen him before. Like it's a clue."

"She did almost seem like she was trying to tell me something." Victoria's voice caught. "I wish I would have asked more questions. But at the time I was afraid she was going to upset Paige with all the talk about missing out on having a dad." Her words broke away, and Owen could feel the heaviness of her emotions weighing on her.

When he closed his eyes to the smiling man in the picture, Owen saw Paige's face, superimposed over the picture of himself at the same age. There it was again, ten years' history taunting him with details he wasn't privy to. Victoria sounded as if she felt guilty about taking Paige away from him. She'd said she'd come back to Fitzgerald Bay so that he could meet his daughter. He had to ask.

"Why did you take so long to come back?"

When he opened his eyes, tears had started leaking down Victoria's face.

"I'm sorry." Her voice shook so much, Owen could hardly make out her words. She gulped a breath and continued in a slightly steadier tone. "I couldn't face you. I couldn't face any of the Fitzgeralds. My dad killed your cousin. He hit him head-on and killed him. People said he might have been drunk."

None of what she'd said was news to Owen, but he got the dreadful sense her words weren't coming out of nowhere. She was building up to something big.

Victoria's lips trembled as she continued. "How could I look any of you in the face? My dad did this horrible, horrible thing."

Owen took a step closer to Victoria and folded his arms around her. There was her old perfume again, pulling him back against irrefutable time into the despair and loss he'd suffered.

"I ran away. I thought I'd give it time, let everyone get calmed down, and then I'd come and find you and tell you."

"So why didn't you?"

Though Victoria had pressed her cheek against his shoulder, clinging to him as she cried, he felt her spine stiffen and she began to pull away.

"Victoria?"

"I thought…" She stumbled backward, shaking her head. "I *knew*. I knew better than to come back, but I believed it would be okay. I thought I could trust you."

Now she wasn't even making sense. "Why did you stay away for ten years?"

Her tear-filled eyes met his. "I was afraid you'd try to take Paige away from me."

Owen felt as though he'd had the breath knocked from him. He tried to think of something to say, but what was there? Yes, he had every right to his daughter, but he'd proved Victoria's fears correct already. He couldn't deny it.

Rather than look at him, Victoria started picking through the broken picture frames they'd moved aside while they swept.

Owen looked at the broken picture frames. It might take all night for Victoria to sort through the mess, and he knew she always rose early to get started with each day's fresh baking.

A tear splashed from Victoria's chin onto the freshly swept floor.

Owen crouched down beside her and picked up a broken picture frame. "Tell you what. I'll clean up. You go check on Paige and make sure she's okay. Take your time."

With a final sniffle, Victoria's footfalls disappeared in the direction of the staircase. Owen didn't watch her go, but took a deep breath, trying to quiet the emotions that raged inside him. His head felt hot and his hands trembled as he reached for the nearest picture, the one of Olivia's parents.

They smiled for the camera, and Owen's eyes narrowed at the face that seemed familiar.

A face that almost looked like his.

He shook that thought away, absurd as it was. He was only about five years older than Olivia, and he'd never been to Ireland. Though he knew that wasn't him in the picture, in some ways, it was.

That man had left his daughter behind, left Olivia

to be raised by a single mother. Had he known about his daughter? Did it matter?

Owen wished he could push aside the vine of guilt that curled around him, but the greedy tendrils only crawled higher.

Everything blurred together.

Olivia's father.

Olivia's baby.

What was it Victoria had said when she'd learned Olivia had a secret baby?

Maybe she was afraid if the baby's father knew about her, he'd try to take her away...if he was from a wealthy family, someone of means and an established reputation, and she was just a poor single girl, with nothing to show. If she had no support network, no income, the baby might have been awarded to the father.

Owen tried to tell himself that Victoria had been talking about Olivia's baby, not her own. But at the same time, he realized exactly why her impromptu hypothesis had sounded so well thought out, so rehearsed.

She'd wrestled with those very fears every day for ten years, hadn't she?

I couldn't face you. I couldn't face any of the Fitzgeralds. My dad killed your cousin.

Her words swirled together, forming a pattern in his mind—a pattern that made sense only when he was willing to look at it from her perspective, not his.

Victoria had feared that his wealthy, powerful family would take away the only family member she had left. She'd hidden Paige from him because she hadn't wanted to lose her.

Suddenly he realized the enormous courage and faith it must have taken for her to return to Fitzgerald Bay at all.

The guilt that had been climbing steadily higher all this time now reached his throat, choking off his breath, sending stars dancing across his vision. He stumbled backward and slumped into a chair.

Victoria's greatest fear had been that he would take Paige away from her, yet she'd risked everything to return to Fitzgerald Bay to tell him the truth.

And then he'd proved her worst fears correct by demanding she share custody.

Owen fought for breath.

What was he doing? What was he thinking? How many times had he wished he could dry Victoria's tears? And yet, this time, he'd been the one to cause them.

Sucking in a slow breath, he struggled to think. Victoria didn't trust his family, and she had no reason to trust him, especially not now. Was there any way he could possibly earn her trust back?

Unsure what his next move should be, Owen got to work cleaning up the mess in the dining room. By the time Victoria returned, Owen had most of the broken glass removed from the frames and had sorted the pictures into stacks for salvaging. Too bad he hadn't been able to sort out the havoc he'd wreaked with her life.

"Paige is asleep." Victoria set a couple of boxes on the table nearest him. "How about if we put the pictures that need new frames in one box, and the frames that need repair in another?"

"Sounds good."

As they worked in silence a few more minutes, Owen's mind spun over the question of what to do. Should he apologize to Victoria for insisting on his parental rights and shared custody?

What if she interpreted that as a sign that he didn't want his daughter? It didn't make sense for him to waffle back and forth until he'd solidly made up his mind on what his next move should be.

Victoria had already told him he needed to earn Paige's trust before revealing that he was her father. Obviously, he needed to work at earning back *her* trust, too. But it seemed like such an insurmountable task, after all he'd done to tear it down.

He hung a couple of undamaged pictures back on the wall, knowing he should be focused on the case and not his personal life. Another thought occurred to him—one that, thankfully, might bring them closer to solving the case, which was what he knew he should be thinking about anyway.

"The fleeing figure I saw this evening—the female? She had blond hair sticking out from underneath her hat. I'm not sure how long it was—long enough to flutter as she went around the corner."

For a moment, Victoria looked shaken. At first Owen thought her response might be due to his sudden change of subject. But then she whispered, "Britney, my waitress, has long blond hair. She would know when we'd have the most money on hand." She shook her head, wincing. "I gave her time off whenever she needed it. I don't get upset when she comes in late. Why would she do this to me?"

"If she wasn't working alone—"

"You think Charlotte put her up to it?" Victoria bit her lip.

"Charlotte turned on the light just in time to scare the intruder away. It could have been a coincidence, but it could also have been a preplanned signal."

"So now what are you going to do? Arrest them? Bring them in for questioning?"

"There's nothing to be gained by that at this point. It would be best not to let on that we suspect them. We don't have any fingerprints, and the footprints I got this evening are too generic to convict anyone."

"So then what? We watch them?"

"We watch them carefully." Owen nodded. "And we wait for them to make their next move."

Victoria exhaled a long, shaky breath. "And we pray that no one gets hurt."

Owen hung the last two undamaged pictures on

the wall. He'd be praying—for Victoria, for Paige and for answers.

With the room finally clean, Owen had no excuse to linger any longer. As he tromped toward the door, he felt far older than he had when he'd come in, and weighed down by so many questions.

The Monday crowd was thin. Victoria would have loved to tell herself it was just a coincidence, possibly a result of last night's snow, but she knew the boarded-over window had to be a turnoff for potential customers. And in spite of her efforts to disguise the damage from the inside, she'd seen a number of folks staring at the closed curtains and whispering.

By the time she brought Paige home from school, the Sugar Plum was empty.

"What can I do to help you, Mom?" Paige asked, scampering back down the stairs after stashing her coat and backpack upstairs in their apartment above the café.

Victoria had heard that question too many times from her daughter in the past week *not* to be suspicious. "Why do you think you need to help me, Paige?"

"I can do things, Mom. I'm not a little kid. I can do work, and then you don't have to pay someone else to do it."

The innocence and good intentions on her daughter's face made Victoria feel even worse. "Paige."

She pulled her little girl into a hug. "You are a child. You deserve the freedom to do little-kid things, not work—"

Paige wrestled out of Victoria's arms. "I'm not a little kid!"

A moment too late, Victoria realized how her words must have sounded to Paige. "That's not what I meant. I just don't want you to feel burdened by everything that's going on."

"Why not? This is my home, too." She stomped past her mom toward the kitchen. "I'll fill the salt and pepper shakers."

Victoria sighed and headed after her, vacillating between keeping Paige from helping—or just giving in and letting her little girl help out, even though it made her feel terribly guilty. "Let me get the salt and pepper for you, then." She handed the big containers to her daughter. "I'm proud of you, that you want to help. It's a very grown-up thing to do. I just don't want you to feel like you *have* to do it."

"You're just afraid I'll mess it up, like I messed up catching the bad guy." Paige took the containers and left the kitchen.

As the last few words floated back behind Paige, Victoria stopped still as though she'd been slapped. Did Paige feel as though she had to make up for letting the bad guy get away? Victoria stared in the direction her daughter had disappeared, weighing what she might say to her, but before she could get her feet moving after her, she heard the bell on the front door jingle.

Finally, a customer.

Victoria hurried to the foyer, eager to wait on whoever had come in.

She looked around the room.

There was no one there.

Victoria stepped into the nearest dining room, but saw only Paige, already getting to work on the salt and pepper shakers.

Odd.

Victoria was sure she'd heard the jangle of the swag of sleigh bells that festooned the main entrance year-round. No one else had been inside the building—Charlotte and Britney weren't scheduled to begin their shifts for over an hour—so someone had to have come in. But where were they?

The guests who'd taken rooms over the weekend had all checked out that morning. But perhaps one of them had come back—maybe they thought they'd left something behind? Victoria darted up the stairs to look.

Heart beating hard, Victoria checked each room while clutching her cell phone. Was she overreacting, or was there reason to be alarmed? All of the rooms appeared to be empty, their beds neatly remade, awaiting the guests who'd already booked for the upcoming Saint Patrick's Day weekend.

Clambering back down the stairs, Victoria was

relieved to see Paige busy at work gathering salt and pepper shakers from all the tables.

"Paige, did you see anyone come in?"

"Nope," Paige called over her shoulder as she headed toward the far end of the dining room.

Victoria saw a shadow move across the window just beyond Paige.

Her heart stopped.

Overreacting. That was all, she was overreacting. She took a deep breath and stared outside the window, willing the shadow to appear again.

There. The distinct movement of a shape beyond the window. A man. A big man.

"Paige." Victoria tried to keep her voice calm. "Honey, come here."

"I'm almost done, Mom. Just give me a second." Paige continued gathering up an armful of the tiny glass containers, heading closer and closer to the window, and possibly toward danger.

"Paige!" Fear filled Victoria's voice, but she didn't care. She scuttled toward her daughter, afraid of alerting the figure beyond the window to the fact that he'd been spotted, but at the same time, zealous for her daughter's safety. "Get away from the window!"

"Why?" Her blue eyes widened with fear.

"The man." Victoria pulled Paige back as the shadow moved again. "Outside the window. We need to call the police."

"It *is* the police, Mom."

"What?" Victoria couldn't make sense out of her little girl's words.

"Outside. The policeman. The one who keeps coming here."

Victoria blinked and looked back behind her. "The man outside the window is a policeman?"

"Yeah. When I came out of the kitchen, he left through the front door."

Had that been the sound of jangling bells she'd heard? "When did he come in?"

Paige shrugged and shifted the little bottles she held cradled in her arms. "You could ask him."

"Good idea." Victoria took a closer look out the window to confirm the shadowy figure wasn't an intruder, and then felt a gust of anger hit her.

Owen Fitzgerald was chopping wood outside their window.

Victoria stomped outside, not even bothering to grab a jacket. The cold wind didn't even slow her down as she charged around the building to the woodpile.

"Just what do you think you're doing?" Victoria planted her hands solidly on her hips and tried to stare Owen down, even though he was many inches taller than her five-foot-eight.

"Chopping wood." Owen split the round log in front of him, then turned to stack it on the growing pile he'd started behind him.

"Outside my window? After all your warnings that

whoever might be lurking outside our windows could be dangerous? You nearly scared me to death!"

"I—" Owen started.

She took a step closer to him. "You've already done more of it than I have."

Owen plunked down the sledgehammer he'd been using and leveled a stare right back at her. "I came inside. It sounded like you and Paige were having an important discussion in the kitchen. I didn't want to interrupt you—"

Victoria had no qualms interrupting him. "You could have poked your head in and let me know you were here."

"You wouldn't have let me do anything for you, then. You already told me not to finish the pile."

His words only made Victoria feel all the more vindicated in her position. "You *knew* I didn't want you doing this, but you still insisted on doing it. What's going on with you?"

Paige's voice carried from the side of the wraparound porch. "What's going on with *you,* Mom? You didn't want me to help, either."

Victoria spun around, surprised by Paige's sudden appearance. "You're not supposed to be outside without a coat on."

"You don't have a coat on."

"That's different. You're a—" Victoria bit her tongue before she could say *little kid.* She already knew that would make Paige only more upset.

"What am I?" Paige insisted.

"You're, uh…" Victoria blew out a long, slow breath. Though she figured she had a right to be upset with Owen, she wasn't going to let that anger carry over to her treatment of her daughter. "You're right. You're right, Paige, if I'm outside, I should have a coat on. I'm going back inside."

"What about *him?*" Paige gestured to Owen.

Victoria wavered. Did her daughter not even know Owen's name? Paige was usually so good at calling grown-ups by their proper titles. Hadn't she bothered to introduce Paige to Owen?

No, she hadn't—because she'd been too worked up by the fact they'd interacted at all.

"*He* is Detective Owen Fitzgerald," Victoria explained to Paige. "And he's wearing a coat, so he can stay outside if he wants."

Owen flashed a disarming smile and approached the porch with his hand extended. "I'm glad to finally be introduced to you."

Paige shook Owen's hand and gave a little curtsy.

The sudden lump in her throat took Victoria by surprise. They made a lovely picture, the two of them, smiling and shaking hands over the porch rail as the late-afternoon sunlight streamed across the yard. It was an image Victoria didn't think she'd ever forget. And maybe she didn't want to forget it, either.

She swallowed back the lump. "Okay, Paige, let's

go back inside. I saved us some day-old double-fudge brownies in the walk-in."

"What about me?" Owen's deep voice prodded gently.

Victoria froze. She'd told Owen he could get to know his daughter. She'd promised, though it tore her apart to think of Owen taking Paige away from her. "You can have a brownie if you want."

He grinned—that same disarming grin he'd flashed earlier—and Victoria felt her heart give a funny lurch.

"I thought I might finish splitting these logs."

Victoria crossed her arms—it *was* quite chilly out. "You don't have to, but I'm not going to stop you." She was determined not to prove Paige's assertion that she had trouble accepting help from others.

"If I stop in for that brownie when I'm finished, can we talk?"

"If the café isn't too busy, sure." Victoria headed back up to the porch, already not looking forward to the conversation she was certain was going to take place. After all, there was very little chance the café was going to be busy, not until after she had the window replaced, and ultimately, not until trouble stopped plaguing the Sugar Plum.

NINE

Owen poked his head into the kitchen and smiled at the sight of Victoria filling bowls with Irish fish chowder. Curls of her golden hair escaped from the pins that had never seemed to be able to hold it all in place—not even back in high school, when they'd dated. He remembered how her silky curls had felt when she'd let him pull the pins out and free her full mane. She had such gorgeous hair.

When Victoria turned and reached for a tray, she spotted him and startled.

"Sorry to spook you. I finished your woodpile."

"You finished *all* of it?"

"Yes."

"You're going to be sore after all that," she warned him as she placed the steaming bowls on the tray, then stepped past him to hand the food off to her waitress.

A flirty comment came to Owen's mind, about the times she'd massaged his sore muscles after football games in high school.

But Owen was pretty sure she wouldn't appreciate

that. If he was going to earn her trust, he'd have to be careful what he did and said.

"Your brownie's in the fridge." She untied her apron and set it aside.

Owen followed her. "Do we have a moment to talk?"

"Looks like it." Victoria's expression fell. "We're not very busy tonight. I was thinking about sending Britney home early, but…" She looked up at him as she opened the fridge door.

With a glance back to make sure the waitress didn't overhear him, Owen whispered, "You don't want to provoke her?"

Victoria bit her lip and looked uncertain. "What do you think I should do?"

A flash of hope shot through him. Victoria wanted his advice? It was a promising sign—as long as he didn't mess it up.

With another glance back over his shoulder, Owen followed her into the fridge and closed the door securely behind them, surprised by the size of the chilled space they entered. Rows of shelves lined the silvery walls, with food organized in neat rows. "If Britney is involved, she's going to have to act again before we can catch her. But I don't like the idea of inviting trouble, not with you and Paige here." He sighed. "I wish I knew the answer."

When Victoria pinched her eyes shut, Owen was reminded of the question she'd asked him before—

about what God was doing, letting all these bad things happen. He went to church every Sunday, but the pastor's words always seemed to float by in the air around him, instead of taking root in his heart. Now he wished he could pluck those words like so many flowers, and offer them to Victoria in a bouquet of hope.

"God knows." Owen wondered, even as he spoke the words, whether they were really true. "God knows who's behind all of this."

Victoria looked up at him, her warm brown eyes simmering with something that looked a lot like trust. "You're right." She held out her hands. "Maybe we should pray about it."

Unable to breathe, Owen dutifully reached for Victoria's hands, his mind spinning. She wanted to *pray* with him?

The moment he closed his fingers over her slender hands, his mind went blank while terror raced unbridled through him. He'd never been any good at praying. Victoria had given him a shot at earning back her trust, but she wanted him to pray with her? He'd blow it for sure! He didn't know how to pray, and as soon as she realized that, she'd see right through him.

"Dear God," he started the prayer, then let out a long sigh. "We need your help." He swallowed. *He* needed help. What was he doing, praying with Victoria in her refrigerator? "We need lots of help. Please, please help us."

Thankfully, Victoria jumped into the prayer. "Dear God, help us to know what to do. We don't know who to trust. It feels like every time we turn around, something bad happens. And Lord—" Victoria's voice grew soft with emotion "—I don't know how I'm going to get through this. I don't know how I'm going to pay to repair the window, and keep this business going. But You know, Lord. Help me to trust You more."

Victoria gave Owen's hands a gentle squeeze, as though prompting him to finish the prayer. Owen's heart beat harder than it had when he was splitting the logs. "Lord, help us trust You," he repeated what Victoria had said. "Please help us. Amen."

When he opened his eyes, he was surprised to see Victoria wiping away tears.

"Thank you." She smiled at him—sincerely smiled—for the first time in over ten years.

Owen felt his heart soar and he had to resist the impulse to pull her into his arms. There had always been a palpable chemistry between them—an irresistible chemistry, as he recalled. With the innocent contact of her hands cupped in his in prayer, Owen felt a deluge of loving feelings smack him with powerful force.

"I, um…" He struggled for words, wanting to act on his growing feelings for her, but he knew he had to proceed cautiously. He'd already damaged everything between them. Rebuilding it would take time. "I was hoping to spend some time with you and Paige today. It's my day off, and you said…"

Worry filled Victoria's face. "I know. I promised."

Owen's heart tore. He hated that the idea of spending time with him would wipe the smile from her face so quickly. But he kept his eyes focused on the goal. He had a daughter to get to know, and he hoped his presence on-site might have the added benefit of giving him a shot at catching their mysterious intruder—or at the very least, keeping the perpetrator at bay.

It took Victoria the better part of the next few days to get used to Owen stopping by. Whether it was for coffee refills, the soup-and-sandwich special or for his extracautious presence hovering about in the evenings, she found herself adjusting to his presence, and felt a foreign stirring inside her when he gave her a twinkle-eyed smile. It would be all too easy to let her old feelings for him resurface.

But at the same time, the mounting sense of dread in her heart told her she'd only found a moment of calm before the storm. They hadn't caught whoever was behind the break-ins. And though Owen was easing into the task of getting to know Paige—they'd explained he was around for extra security, and Paige hadn't questioned them—Victoria knew the day would come when Owen would demand she fulfill her promise to split their daughter's time between them.

Victoria wasn't sure how she could ever do that. Paige had never spent one night away from her.

Rather than worry about it, though, as she rolled out crusts for the Irish meat and potato pies that were her Wednesday-night special, Victoria prayed.

And nearly jumped in the air when Owen walked through the back door of her kitchen.

"You nearly scared me to death!" She swung her rolling pin in his general direction, missing him by several feet. "In case you'd forgotten, I'm still a bit jumpy. And—" she dropped her voice and took a step closer to him, just in case Charlotte was within hearing distance "—until we catch whoever's been causing trouble around here, I'm sure I'll stay jumpy."

Owen's blue eyes sparkled mischievously. "I've solved one mystery, anyway."

Intrigued, Victoria set down her rolling pin. "Which one?"

But instead of a straight answer, Owen raised one finger to his lips. "This way." He led her on tiptoe to the back door, silently opening it just a crack.

Leaning close to Owen and poking her head around past his arm, Victoria was able to see where he pointed.

Paige crouched on the small patio just beyond the back door, nose to nose with the scrawny calico cat that'd been coming by.

And now Victoria understood why. "She's feeding it," she whispered. "Do you think it's safe? What if it's carrying rabies?"

"It looks friendly enough. Rabid animals don't tend to be so friendly."

Victoria pulled her head back inside. "She's been asking for a cat. I didn't think it would be a good idea, with us living right above the restaurant. But if I had to choose, I'd rather have a house cat than let Paige run after strays. What do you think?"

"I'm no expert on cats."

"But you're her—" Victoria caught herself. She knew Owen was Paige's father, but they hadn't discussed the details of their arrangement, such as making decisions about pets. Would Owen butt heads with her over the details of his daughter's life? What if they fought over everything and upset Paige? Suddenly the future stretched out before her like a heavy, choking blanket of uncertainty.

Though the two of them had stepped inside, Owen's arm remained on the door behind her, creating a protected alcove of just the two of them. But Victoria felt that space growing smaller as Owen lowered his head closer to hers.

She raised her hands to hold him back. Their relationship was complicated enough. She didn't need *feelings* getting in the mix, too. But every time she was around him, she felt the old pull she'd thought she'd left behind ten years before. The more time she spent around him, the more difficult it became to ignore those feelings. It would be so easy to step right back into the romantic relationship they'd once shared.

His shoulders came to rest against the palms of her hands. Victoria opened her mouth to protest, to tell him to back away, but all she managed was a breathless, "Owen."

The tip of his nose touched her forehead, and his lips grazed her eyebrows, planting tiny whispers of kisses there. All the walls she'd tried to put up to keep him away fell brick by brick as he nuzzled his way closer into her heart.

"Owen." She tightened her grip on his shoulders. How many times during his recent visits had she wanted to be in his arms again? With all the uncertainties in her life, she could use a comforting presence, and someone to hold her close and tell her everything was going to be all right.

But Owen wasn't that person. Owen wasn't going to make everything all right, he was going to take Paige away from her.

But it felt so good to be close to him, to feel his solid muscles supporting her.

His eyes slid into focus in front of hers, twin blue pools of caring and strength.

She gulped a breath to clear her head, but all she got was a taste of him lingering in the air so close. His hands slid farther around her, pulling her against him. She looked him full in the face and her lips parted.

His kiss was gentle. The terrors and stress of the past few weeks melted away, and she was eighteen again, in love with Owen for the very first time. She closed her eyes, wanting the moment to last forever, wishing it could be real.

The sound of little boots stomping on the stoop outside snapped Victoria back to attention. Just in time, she and Owen broke away.

Paige stepped inside, practically in between them, her smile broadening when she saw the detective. "Hi!" She greeted him on her way to the hand-washing sink. "Detective Owen Fitzgerald." She worked her hands up into a soapy lather, just as Victoria had taught her.

Victoria caught her breath. Should she say something to Paige about the cat? She couldn't seem to think straight after being in Owen's arms. And she couldn't look at him again, either. Instead, she got in line behind Paige at the sink, washed her hands and returned to her work with the pie crust. Irish meat-and-potato pies didn't bake themselves. Whatever else was going on at the Sugar Plum, she had to keep the place afloat.

Paige dried her hands on a towel and looked Owen up and down. "Detective Owen Fitzgerald," she repeated in a singsong tone, then scowled.

Still a little self-conscious from nearly being caught in an embrace with Owen, Victoria laughed at her daughter's funny face. "What are you doing, Paige? I hope you're being polite to the detective."

"I'm trying to remember." Paige hung the hand towel back on its rack. *"Hmm, hmm."*

Owen planted his hands on his knees and crouched down closer to her level. "What are you trying to remember?"

But Paige only shook her head, her curling blond ponytails flapping side-to-side with the movement. "Can people hum and sing at the same time?"

"I suppose," Owen said with a chuckle. "If they don't know the words very well. Or if they're trying not to sing out loud. Why?"

"Detective Owen Fitzgerald," Paige sang the name softly, then scowled again. "It's not quite right."

"Are you writing a song about me?"

"Not me—the man who broke into the safe. He was humming." Paige hummed a few more notes, snapped her fingers and then finished in tune with "Owen Fitzgerald."

Owen hummed the notes back to her.

Before he'd finished, Victoria named the song. "'The Wreck of the Edmund Fitzgerald.'"

"No, Mom." Paige sang the words. "The wreck of the *Owen* Fitzgerald."

"It's a song, Paige," Victoria corrected. "The name of the song is 'The Wreck of the Edmund Fitzgerald.'"

"But he wasn't singing *Edmund.*" Paige shook her head emphatically and sang again, more forcefully this time, "The wreck of the Owen Fitzgerald."

Owen quickly shushed her. "*My* name?" He looked a little concerned. "Why would the person breaking into *your* safe sing *my* name?"

"Maybe it wasn't your name." Paige headed for the stairs that led to their apartment, clearly tired of the conversation. "Maybe it just sounded like your name. He was only partly singing and partly humming. I didn't *really* hear the words."

Once Paige had left, Owen turned to Victoria and raised an eyebrow.

Victoria looked out into the foyer to be sure they weren't going to be overheard. Charlotte and Britney weren't scheduled to come in until five, but Victoria still wanted to be careful. "That complicates matters," she told Owen in a hushed tone once she was sure no one else was listening in.

"The singing?"

"Yes. Remember Clint, Britney's on-again, off-again boyfriend you caught peeking in the window? I know Paige said he wasn't the man who broke into the safe, but now I'm not so sure."

"Does he sing?"

"Yes. He and Britney both sing. They're aspiring entertainers—singing and acting. That's how they met."

"But why would he be singing *my* name?"

Victoria had to think about it. "Have you ever pulled him over, or issued him a parking ticket?"

"It's possible, but why would he break into *your* safe if he was upset with *me?*"

Victoria set another pile of dough on the rolling surface and gave it a couple of good, angry rolls. Nothing like a little extra gumption to get her pie crusts flaky thin. "If he was upset with you, and if Britney has something against me, and the two of them are working together—maybe they thought they could both get even with us at once."

"Maybe." Owen walked closer to where Victoria was working. "I'd have to check my records." He hovered over her shoulder.

Lifting a crust onto the waiting pan, Victoria turned in one motion to face Owen. "What?"

His face held tenderness. "I'd forgotten how much I missed you."

Her heart started hammering inside her, the memory of the kiss they'd shared still too fresh, and far too tempting to repeat. "We're not in high school anymore," she reminded him. "Life is really complicated now."

"What are you saying?"

Victoria had to set down the rolling pin again. She didn't know when she was ever going to get the pies made. "I'm saying that I'm watching my employees to try to figure out if they're conspiring to steal against me, and bracing myself against the possibility of another break-in. And Olivia's murderer is still on the loose. And you're asking me to share my child. I'm saying, life is really complicated right now, and I don't know if I can handle any more complications."

"So, I'm a complication?"

Picking up her rolling pin, she waved it at him, as

much to get him to back off as anything. "You're a detective. But when you kiss me…" She took a scattered breath and started flattening the next pile of dough. "*Then* you're a complication."

Owen didn't leave, but quietly watched as she placed the rolled pastry crust smoothly over the waiting pans and flattened the next mound of soft dough.

She glanced up at him, then went back to rolling her dough, reminding herself that it didn't matter one bit what her feelings might be for Owen. He would be a part of her life from now on—because they would share responsibility for raising Paige.

But as Paige came downstairs with a board game and asked Owen to play, and the two of them trotted out to the dining room together, Victoria realized it did matter. She had feelings for the detective, feelings she needed to get under control before she did something crazy—like kiss him again.

Owen blinked at the red numbers on his bedside clock: 12:52.

Normally he was exhausted after his evening shift ended, and had no trouble falling asleep. Tonight he had too many things on his mind.

The guilt he felt about the circumstances surrounding Victoria continued to grow, gnawing at him, preventing him from closing his eyes.

Had it been a mistake to kiss her?

He couldn't decide. The kiss itself was the kind of

thing any man might search his whole life to find. Kissing Victoria was better than eating anything she'd ever baked, and that was saying something. But kissing Victoria only left him wanting to kiss her more, and that was craziness.

She'd called him a complication. She'd waved her rolling pin at him as if she might clobber him with it if he got any closer.

But she hadn't clobbered him with it. She'd kissed him back.

She had feelings for him, he was nearly certain of it, but she didn't trust him because he'd asked for joint custody of Paige. She was nervous about what that meant, what it *could* mean.

He'd thought about calling Cooper and telling him to cancel the case, but how could he give up such hard-fought territory?

What if she didn't feel the same way about him that he felt about her? What if giving up his demands at this point didn't restore her trust? What if he gave up his rights to Paige, and then Victoria ran off with his daughter, and he never saw her again?

Owen pounded his pillow flat, wishing he could so easily smooth out all the wrinkles of the past. The biggest problem, of course, was the past ten years. They'd been blissfully in love back in high school. He could imagine himself being in love with her once again, except for the betrayals that had passed between them.

Her father had killed his cousin. Though the

Fitzgeralds were polite to Victoria, he knew from comments such as those Ryan had made in the office the week before that they still associated Victoria with their cousin's death.

So, even if he could convince Victoria that *he* didn't blame her, that his love for her was bigger than the hurt of the past ten years, that didn't erase the looming specter of his family's condemnation. Whenever she looked at him, she had to see the angry eyes of the whole Fitzgerald clan glaring at her over his shoulders, blaming her for Patrick's death. Guilty by association.

Even if he loved Victoria, that didn't change the way his family felt about her.

Throwing back the covers with a disgusted grunt, he wrestled running shoes onto his feet and grabbed a jacket. Pounding his pillow hadn't helped. Maybe pounding the pavement would.

The bluffs of Fitzgerald Bay provided a vigorous workout, and the empty streets made for a clear track. He ran up and down each block in turn, sprinting on the downhill stretches, plodding back up and sprinting down again.

Finally he stood, breathless, outside the Sugar Plum Café, and looked up at the historical landmark with its dark windows unblinking against the night, and wondered what secrets lay within. Was the Sugar Plum being targeted because of some secret linked to Olivia's death? Or did the peculiar song Paige had overheard the robber singing actually point somehow to a link to the Fitzgerald family?

He circled slowly around the building, pondering. Had he missed a clue somewhere? Was there something more he could do to catch the culprit? Pausing to restack a few of the logs he'd split, he arranged them in a stable-looking pile and wished everything in his world could be so easily fixed.

Then he ambled back around the backside of the house, pausing to stomp the dirt from his shoes when he reached the sidewalk.

A sound caught his attention. In the split second it took him to lift his head and look up, a dark figure jumped out of the night, landing on him and knocking him to the ground.

TEN

Victoria ran out the back door with a bright flashlight and shone it on the spot where the police officer had tackled the man to the ground.

Finally, they'd caught the shadowy figure she'd seen from the Sugar Plum windows.

The officer wrestled the man upright. She immediately recognized the uniformed officer who'd captured the criminal. Hank Monroe. Normally she didn't like the man, but if he'd caught her assailant and finally brought peace to her household, she'd forgive him for every harsh thing he'd ever said.

Hank wrestled the fighting figure around until he faced her, and the bright beam of her flashlight shone on his face.

"Owen?"

He looked furious but had stopped fighting Hank.

"Owen Fitzgerald." Hank yanked him around and pulled out a set of handcuffs. "Aah, the pieces are starting to fall into place now. Why didn't I realize it sooner?"

Owen blinked against the light of Victoria's flashlight. "Let me guess. You saw someone hanging around and called the police?"

Victoria took a step closer as Hank slapped the cuffs on Owen's wrists. "You're the one who told me to call right away if I saw anyone."

As the metal cuffs locked tightly around his wrists, Owen hung his head. His mouth fell open as though he couldn't quite believe what was happening, but he couldn't think of what to say in his defense.

Hank gave him a hard jerk in the direction of the police station.

"Wait." Victoria stepped closer. "Owen *can't* be the perpetrator. He was on duty all the times I've had trouble before. He was the officer who responded to my calls."

"I'm *not* the perpetrator," Owen stated bluntly, glaring at Hank.

"Oh, no?" Hank chuckled icily. "It all makes too much sense. Of course *you* were the first officer on the scene. You were already there because you *committed* the crime. That's why the perp always got away. It's like Clark Kent and Superman. You never see them in the same room at the same time, because they're the same guy." He continued to shove Owen in the direction of the police station.

Victoria placed a hand on Hank's shoulder. "Owen isn't the perpetrator, Hank."

Hank's brown eyes settled on hers. "How do you know?"

Victoria looked back and forth between Owen and Hank.

Two men with so much in common. She'd gone to school with both of them, dated both of them, though Hank just once, and returned to town to find both of them still single. They both came from prominent, well-respected families. Why did she trust Owen over Hank?

Had she misjudged them both?

How *did* she know?

"I just don't think Owen would do that."

Hank's eyes glinted in the darkness. "That doesn't make him innocent. I'll be back in a minute to take your statement. You might want to go inside and make sure he didn't do any damage."

As Hank hauled Owen off in the direction of the police station, Victoria hurried inside, Hank's words a reminder that she'd left her daughter sleeping quietly in bed.

Paige slumbered silently on, and Victoria leaned against her door frame, listening to the even sound of her daughter's breathing. How many hundreds of times when Paige was a baby had Victoria watched her sleeping, listening for those peaceful breaths that sometimes came so silently?

Owen had never had that experience.

Her heart pinched. Owen couldn't possibly be guilty. Hank had made a valid point, though, and Victoria couldn't think how to refute it. And Owen hadn't really fought Hank. Was it because, as an officer of the law, he knew he'd only get himself into trouble by resisting arrest, and that the best thing to do was go quietly and let his innocence be proved later?

Or was it because he did have something to hide?

Faintly, she heard a knock at the door and hurried down to see Hank standing in the doorway. He was smiling broadly. The sight was a tad unnerving.

"I need to get a statement from you about what you saw, and confirm that you want to press charges."

"I don't know. I'm not convinced Owen—"

But Hank didn't let her finish. "Don't you see, Victoria? This is your shot to end all your troubles. If Owen goes to prison—"

"Prison?"

Hank's expression softened. "He stole three thousand dollars from you. He busted your window. He's been stalking you at night. Yeah, I'd say he's going to go to prison." Hank smiled with a little too much confidence. A little too much happiness.

Why in the world was Hank so pleased with the idea of his fellow officer going to prison? She shook her head. "I'm not going to press charges. I don't believe he's guilty of anything."

"But you've got to," Hank snarled.

"No—" Victoria took a step back across her threshold, her mind made up "—I don't." She closed the door quickly and snapped the lock shut, praying it would keep Hank out.

Something wasn't right about Hank's reaction. In fact, the more she thought about it, the more she realized that there were a lot of things about Hank that didn't sit well with her. She needed to talk to Owen.

Business was slow the next morning when Owen walked in, the blue of his eyes overshadowed by the dark circles around them. His T-shirt looked rumpled and his jeans had a hole in the knee. He ordered coffee and a Cape Cod egg scramble, one of her signature specialties made with local crab meat, asparagus, avocado and plenty of asiago cheese.

She brought him the plate as he nursed his coffee in a booth in the corner.

Since no more customers had arrived, she set the plate in front of him and sat down in the opposite seat.

"I didn't do it." His expression was completely flat, save for the weariness in his heavy eyes.

"How did you get out of jail?"

"Ryan paid my bail. Then he gave me a lecture I won't soon forget."

Victoria winced. The eldest Fitzgerald brother was an imposing figure, and she'd always been a bit intimidated by him.

As Owen settled in eating his breakfast in silence, Victoria studied his face.

When he finished, Owen patted his lips with a napkin and settled it over his plate with a sigh. "It's up to you to decide if you want to press charges."

"I'll press charges," Victoria said evenly, "when I believe the right man has been caught."

Hope sparkled in Owen's eyes.

"I realized when I saw Hank's badge last night what a stupid mistake I'd made, and how obviously guilty I looked. If I could figure out a clear reason why you should believe I'm innocent, I'd give it to you." He leaned back and made a pained face. "It's like the situation with Charles, with people thinking he killed Olivia. I don't want to believe my brother would do that. I'd defend him to the death, but at the same time, I've taken a vow to see justice served, and my feelings for my brother don't make him innocent. Until we have clear evidence one way or the other, we just don't know."

She mulled his words, still puzzling through the mess. "I've been thinking about why Hank was gloating last night. What I still don't understand about Hank is why he's never said anything to clear up the rumor that I ran away with him."

Owen's head snapped up and he met her eyes.

"He's got to have heard the rumors about Paige being his daughter," Victoria continued, "but I've never heard him deny them."

"You didn't deny them." Owen let the words fall slowly, thoughtfully.

"Because I didn't think people would believe me. But Hank's a police officer, and his father was a judge. If he denied the rumors, that would be the end of it." She shrugged. "Unless he *has* denied them, and they just refuse to die down."

"No." Owen shook his head. "I've never heard of Hank denying any of it. In fact—" he rose and picked up his plate "—as I recall, Hank stood by the rumors. That's part of what convinced me to believe them in the first place."

Victoria stood, as well, shaking her head. "But he knows the truth. He knows that Paige couldn't possibly be his. I never let him touch me. And I hadn't seen him since graduation, until Paige and I moved back to town six months ago."

Anger flashed in Owen's eyes. "Hank knows Paige can't possibly be his, but he still perpetuates the rumors that the two of you ran away together years ago. Why?"

Victoria took Owen's plate from him and hurried off toward the kitchen.

Unsure whether he was welcome to follow, Owen took his time leaving the dining room, still puzzling over all the unresolved questions in his life of late. He paused to look at the walls, the pictures a bit sparse since Victoria had rehung them, minus the ones that had been damaged. The picture of him with Patrick now hung at eye level. Owen studied their chocolate milk-topped smiles, wishing he could go back in time to those simple days when he and his cousin had talked about any and everything that was on their minds. He wished he could talk to Patrick again.

"Patrick," he whispered to the empty room. "Why did you have to die?" In the distance he could hear the clatter of Victoria busy in the kitchen, and knew the answer. Her father had hit Patrick head-on.

The memory burned his throat. Victoria had made her father promise he wouldn't drink and drive. She'd begged him to stop drinking entirely, or at the very least, not to drive when he'd been drinking. She'd told him her dad had promised.

Someone had lied.

Owen headed out the door and across the street to the police station. He wasn't scheduled to work for the next two days—wasn't even sure they'd have him back after that, depending on what kind of fuss Hank might make. But if Victoria wasn't pressing charges, there was no reason anyone had to believe he'd done anything wrong.

Instead of heading for his desk, he made a beeline for the file room where the records on old cases were kept. His fingers found the file on the wreck that had killed Patrick.

He laid it out on the table, pictures spilling forth from their ten-year-old tomb as though they'd been there only a day. The memories were just as fresh, though Owen had never looked at the file before. His gut clenched at the sight of Patrick's blue T-Bird, in which he'd ridden with Patrick many times, reduced to a mangled ball of metal, crunched almost beyond recognition.

And Victoria's father's truck, a two-ton rust bucket of solid steel, its front end crumpled like a red paper ball, the back three-quarters utterly unscathed. Owen blinked and shuffled through the pictures.

Was the back end of Stanley Evans's pickup truck really unscathed? A white streak, which looked almost like glare from the camera flash, stretched most of the length of the vehicle.

Owen squinted at a couple of closer images. It wasn't glare at all, but paint, with corresponding scratches and a stretch of indentation indicating Stanley Evans's vehicle had scraped alongside something white. Thinking back through ten years of fog, Owen tried to recall if he'd ever seen the scrape on the truck before. He'd been over to Victoria's plenty of times in the days and weeks leading up to the accident. Stanley Evans's truck had almost always been parked outside.

And hadn't he and Victoria washed her car on a sunny day not long before the accident? And then, because he wanted an excuse to spend more time with her, Owen had suggested they wash her father's vehicle.

The white scrape *hadn't* been there then.

Owen carried the file into his father's office.

Though he wasn't looking forward to facing his dad after the events of the night before, he needed answers. The pounding in his heart told him so.

He balanced the pictures on the open file and knocked on the chief's door with his other hand.

Aiden Fitzgerald looked up, and a guarded smile spread across his face as he recognized his son. "Didn't expect to see you today. Come in."

Owen sat opposite his dad's desk and placed the pictures in front of him. As he might have expected, before Aiden asked him the reason for his visit, his father had a few things to say to him first.

"You got yourself in quite a fix last night. Hank Monroe is convinced you're behind all the trouble at the Sugar Plum."

"That's preposterous." Owen gave his dad a challenging look. Leave it to the old man to sort out right from wrong. He'd been doing it for most of his life.

"You have an alibi for the other incidents?"

"I was on duty during most of them."

"You were the first man on the scene. Hank thinks that's more than a coincidence."

Owen sighed. He was never going to get a chance to ask his father about the pictures in Patrick's file at this rate. "I wouldn't do anything to hurt Victoria." He stared his father down, daring him to suggest otherwise.

"Is that a fact?" Fitzgerald blue eyes bored into his. "Never?"

"Never."

Aiden glanced at the pictures Owen had placed on his desk. "Even though her father killed your cousin?"

"Did Monroe bring up that detail?"

"He didn't need to. I see it's on your mind, as well." Aiden's eyes darted from the pictures and back to his son. "So what's this intrusion about? Looking for peace? Try going to church."

"I'm always in church on Sundays."

"Yes." Weariness clouded Aiden's eyes. "But are you listening?"

Owen dropped his father's gaze and instead studied the pictures. Was he listening to Pastor Larch every Sunday? He tried to listen, but the words seemed to sweep past him without ever snagging hold of anything. He'd slammed the door on his heart when Patrick had died and Victoria had left him. Not much got past the barrier he'd erected.

"I came to ask you a question."

"I'm listening."

"These white streaks on Stanley Evans's truck—do we know how they got there?"

Aiden's chest rose and fell with a heavy sigh. "We tried to look into it ten years ago. Never got an answer. His daughter left town before we could ask if she knew where her dad had picked up the scrapes. Best theory we could come up with was that, being drunk all the time, he'd swerved and scraped something, and it was never reported. We'll probably never know what it was."

"So no one ever followed up with Victoria?"

"She left town right after the accident. Didn't come back until six months ago."

"I see." Owen stood. "Maybe it's time we ask her, then."

Aiden frowned as though he doubted Victoria would remember anything after ten years, but he didn't call him back.

Owen carried the pictures across the street to where Victoria pulled bubbling fruit tarts from her ovens. He breathed in the aroma of apples, blueberries and cherries. "Smells amazing in here."

She gave him a wary look, never really lifting her gaze from the tarts she balanced on their way to the cooling racks. She transferred the last two pans before switching the oven off and turning her attention to him. "Can I help you?"

"I hope so." Owen gingerly laid out the pictures on the pristinely clean countertop.

Victoria's face blanched as she looked over his shoulder. "Is that—?"

"Your father's truck." Owen nodded. "Or what was left of it after the accident. This is the file—"

"Why are you looking at that? Why dredge up the past?"

"I need answers."

"*I* need answers about who's been causing trouble today, not ten years ago." She took a step back. "I told you I was sorry, Owen. If I could change what happened, I would."

Owen could see she was upset, and probably about to throw him out, and maybe even change her mind about pressing charges. "Did your father have an accident prior to *the* accident?" He blurted the question quickly.

"I don't know."

"There's white paint on his truck. It wasn't there that day when we washed his truck—how long before the accident was that? A couple of weeks?"

Victoria raised her hand to her forehead, her face flushed, whether from the steaming tarts or anger or something else, he wasn't sure. "It was the Saturday before. I remember because I felt nauseous but I didn't know why. I was already pregnant—I just didn't know."

Her blush made sense.

But the timing didn't.

"That was less than a week before the accident. Not much time for him to pick up damage like this—"

"Especially when you consider he wasn't driving at all that week."

Owen looked Victoria in the eye. "Wasn't driving?"

"No. Remember? He promised me he wouldn't drink and drive. He couldn't stop drinking, so that truck sat in that spot until..." She swallowed.

"Until the night of the accident?"

"I think so."

Owen stared at the pictures. "So, maybe it wasn't an accident?"

"What?"

"Patrick's car was blue. Your father's truck was red. They were on a country road—there was nothing white to scrape up against, except maybe for another car."

"So, what are you saying? Do you think—"

Owen didn't have to think. He knew. "Someone else caused the accident."

Victoria shook her head. "But my father was behind the wheel of the truck that hit Patrick. He caused the accident."

Realizing that Victoria didn't have his law enforcement background, he pointed to the pictures and explained his theory. "When I investigate an accident, I determine who or what caused the accident based on the factors that created the situation that led to the accident."

"In this case, my dad driving drunk."

"No." Owen flipped open the file to the toxicology report. "Everyone in town always assumed he was drunk because of his reputation, but according to this, there was no alcohol in his system when he died."

Victoria froze. "He promised me he wasn't going to drink and drive anymore."

"I have every reason to believe he didn't break that promise." Owen pulled out the photograph of the white streak on the truck. "Someone else grazed your father's vehicle. That's what caused this white streak. It wasn't there when we washed the truck the week before. He didn't drive it again until that night, so he couldn't have picked it up between then and the accident."

"And he wasn't drunk when he was driving." Victoria spoke the words as though she was still trying to convince herself they were true.

"Somebody else scraped against his truck—somebody in a white vehicle. They forced his truck to crash into Patrick's car. Your dad didn't cause that accident. Somebody in a white car caused the accident that killed them both."

It took Victoria's wide brown eyes almost a full minute to blink. "But who?"

ELEVEN

Victoria's thoughts were full over the next couple of days.

Maybe her father *hadn't* killed Patrick.

It changed everything.

It changed nothing.

Patrick was still dead and so was her father. She and Owen agreed not to say anything to anyone about their discovery. Whoever had actually caused the accident that day had believed for the past ten years that they'd gotten away with their crime. If they learned otherwise, they might try to silence those who knew the truth.

Owen had insisted they not take that risk.

They tried to recall everyone who drove a white vehicle ten years before, but the color had been as ubiquitous as snow in winter. The accident could have been cause by anyone.

Besides, it wasn't as though Victoria had any time to discuss the past with anyone. She had a future to take care of, and her best hope of turning a profit for the month of March lay in a little present from God: Saint Patrick's Day was on a Saturday this year.

The annual Fitzgerald Bay Saint Patrick's Day Irish Heritage Parade and Festival was always a big deal, but even more so since the holiday fell on a weekend. The inn was booked almost full, and though the weather was forecast to be chilly, for once it wasn't supposed to rain or snow. That meant there was a potential for huge crowds lining the parade route that went right past the front of the Sugar Plum. And given the predicted chill in the air, Victoria was planning a full lineup of hot coffees, cocoas and teas. And, of course, Irish pastries to go with them.

And then, in the evening, the Sugar Plum would host a buffet of corned beef, red potatoes, cabbage and all the trimmings. Victoria would prepare most of the food ahead of time so she could focus on busing tables, which would hopefully be filled for hours.

If that wasn't enough to keep her thoughts occupied, Paige would be riding on the church float with her Sunday school class. And since the girl insisted on wearing her green dress again—Owen had told her how nice she looked in it, so she wanted to wear it again—Victoria had the added hassle of figuring out how many layers of thick tights and long underwear she could stuff under Paige's dress.

So really, she had little time to think about whether the mysterious intruder who'd been breaking into the

Sugar Plum might return, or who had actually caused the accident that had killed Patrick and her father.

But Owen had clearly had time to think about it.

He popped his head into her kitchen around closing time Friday evening.

"I see you got your new safe." He gestured with the papers he held in his hands.

"It's punch-proof." Victoria shot him a quick smile before turning her attention to the pans of shamrock-shaped cookies she was frosting. She'd made five times the usual number, and hoped to sell each one, though any leftovers would end up on the evening buffet. "What have you got there?"

"I printed off a map of the roads in the area where the accident took place."

He didn't specify which accident. He didn't need to.

Victoria stopped frosting cookies, quickly washed her hands and ushered him out to the front podium, where a bright light would illuminate what he needed her to see.

"Where's Paige?" Owen laid out the pages.

"In her room, reading the books she got at the Reading Nook with the gift certificate from your father. I don't like leaving her up there alone, but she has her cell phone, and I hooked up her old baby monitor so I can hear if there's a disturbance. Every once in a while I hear her laughing at her book, so that calms my fears." She studied the pages as she spoke, unsure what she was supposed to be looking for.

Owen tapped a red X on the page, just inside the Fitzgerald Bay city limits. "I marked the site of the accident. Patrick was headed north to pick up some friends who lived out of town."

"So you're wondering what my father might have been doing driving around out there?"

"He didn't pick up that paint out of thin air. Do you have any idea why he left the house that evening?"

"I was working here." Victoria had been a waitress at the Sugar Plum throughout most of high school. "I was supposed to close that night—back then the Sugar Plum didn't close on Fridays until midnight, and then we had all the cleanup before we could leave. But the police called my aunt after the accident and she drove to town to tell me what happened. She took me to stay with her and my uncle in New York." The memories—her despair, horror and utter mortification, came flooding back.

"And your father hadn't been driving anywhere? Did you need anything that he might have gone to pick up? Groceries? Milk?"

"Dad didn't drink milk. He drank—" She looked at the map, and suddenly knew exactly where her father might have been headed. "He drank moonshine." She tapped the map, where a winding line bisected the other not far beyond the red X. "Frank Gallagher lived right down Mayflower Road."

"Gallagher was finally arrested for running shine, what, about a year after the accident? But he'd been at it for years before the county sheriff caught him."

They both tipped their heads over the spot, and Victoria silently read the names of the people who lived in the area, who would have had a reason to drive the same road that night.

"Murtagh." Victoria tapped the label on a nearby property.

"Where have I heard that last name before?"

"Britney Murtagh, my waitress."

"The blond-haired girl who had means and opportunity to mess with your safe?"

"And maybe a motive, too." Victoria sighed. "Do you think she was hoping to run me out of business so I'd leave town before I stumbled upon the truth of what really happened that night?"

"She'd have been a little kid, but her dad, Larry, has lived on that stretch of road for years. Wonder what he might have been up to that would have prompted him to run your father off the road."

Owen had moved close to Victoria as they both bent their heads over the maps, studying Mayflower Road as though the secrets of what had happened there ten years before might be revealed if only they looked hard enough. Now he met her eyes from only inches away, and Victoria felt the pull of his presence, drawing her closer like a magnet. It would be so easy to dip her head those last two inches and rest her cheek on his shoulder. And she knew how safe and warm she'd feel if he wrapped his arms around her.

The look in his eyes said he *would* wrap his arms around her if she rested her cheek on his shoulder. The old pull of attraction felt stronger every time she looked at him.

Paige's laughter burst from the baby monitor in the kitchen as she giggled at her book upstairs.

Victoria took a step back. Now was not the time to get close to Owen. There were too many uncertainties swirling around them for her to get caught up in the attraction between them. She had her daughter's well-being to think about.

"I need to lock up." Victoria pulled her keys from her pocket and headed for the front door. "And I need to run tonight's report, tuck Paige into bed and then frost about forty dozen more cookies." She waved him toward the door, hoping he'd leave quickly so she could get on with her work.

Owen stepped forward, then hesitated. "I suppose the cookie-frosting has to be done by a pastry-chef professional?"

She squinted at him, unsure what his remark meant.

He gave her a sheepish grin. "I don't have a whole lot of experience frosting cookies, but if you're willing to accept help from a nonprofessional..."

Victoria's heart stumbled. Uncertain as she was whether she ought to spend any time around him, she knew she'd be up most of the night if she didn't have help. With an extra set of hands, the cookies could be done in half the time. "You really don't need to." She paused. Owen looked prepared to leave.

Was she crazy? She couldn't kick him out—not when she knew she could use his help.

"Paige was just getting after me for insisting on doing everything myself. Maybe I could use your help."

"Let's get to work."

She got Owen started with the icing, then ran her cash report and went up to tuck Paige into bed. Owen looked as though he wanted to ask to help with bedtime, but Victoria didn't give him time to speak the words. She and Owen had yet to work out any sort of plan for how they'd arrange joint custody. She wanted to put off that conversation as long as possible.

When she came back downstairs, she found Owen had abandoned the frosting knife for an industrial-size serving spoon, which dripped with bright green frosting. When her eyes widened at the sight, he looked sheepish.

"It's not quite as precise, but it holds enough frosting to do six cookies between dips. Saves time." He frosted four more cookies as he spoke, and nodded to the full pan he'd finished while she was upstairs. "They don't have to be perfect, do they?"

Victoria looked at the cookies he'd finished. No, they weren't quite the works of art she was used to preparing, but they looked plenty festive. And Owen was cranking them out in a fraction of the time it usually took to do the job. She laughed wearily. "You're a genius." Grabbing a full-size spoon from the row of hooks above the island, she joined him. "Show me how you do that."

He smiled—and it lit up her heart more than she wanted.

The crowd gathered for the celebration bright and early the next morning. Owen strode through the crowded streets toward the Sugar Plum with his head tucked low into the collar of his coat. The March wind blasted cold, but at least the sun had poked out. The throng of revelers didn't appear to be letting the chill put a damper on their fun, either. Not only were the streets filled with people, but many of them had kept with the tradition of donning green and white face paint to celebrate the holiday.

Half a dozen young men streaked down the street, wearing nothing above their jeans but green and white paint. Owen shivered on their behalf. He and his cousin Patrick had always talked about painting themselves for the holiday. Their mothers had refused to let them try it, and once Patrick was gone, the appeal of their plan had gone with him.

He reached the Sugar Plum and made it halfway up the steps before catching up to the rear of the line. From the glimpse he got of Victoria through the window, she had her hands full.

Instead of waiting in line and watching her toil through the window, Owen ducked around to the back door, let himself in through the kitchen entrance and washed his hands before joining Victoria at the counter.

She didn't see him, but when the customer ordered two coffee-and-shamrock-cookie specials, Owen noticed the pan in the glass case was down to one cookie. He'd passed the waiting pans in the kitchen, and ducked back to get one.

Victoria spun around just as he returned. The surprise on her face was quickly replaced by a relieved smile. As she pulled out the empty pan and swapped it out for the full one, she warned him, "I don't want you to think I'm going to give you a job here just because you insist on hanging around."

"It's a popular place today."

"It is." She beamed and handed the customer his order.

"Where's Paige?" Owen asked in a whisper as Victoria counted out change for the next customer.

"In the expert care of her Sunday school teachers. I'm hoping to catch a break in time to watch her float go by."

Owen felt an odd swelling in his chest. He'd always loved watching the floats in the parade, and the Sunday school float was a favorite, dating back to when he was a kid. How many years had he wistfully wondered what it would be like to watch his own child on that float?

He'd finally get the chance.

But if it came down to it, he'd let Victoria watch, and cover the store if he had to. The woman had probably been up since three or four that morning, if the fresh-baked pastries that had appeared overnight meant anything. She'd earned a moment's joy to celebrate like everyone else, and he was determined to see that she got it.

Though people continued to pour through the doors right up until the parade's start time of ten o'clock, once the Fitzgerald Bay High School band marched by, the crowd took to the streets, and even those who'd been soaking up the warmth of the woodstoves in the Sugar Plum dining rooms headed outside to watch the festivities.

Charlotte and Britney nearly pushed Victoria out the door.

"The Sunday school float is always near the front of the parade. You'd better get out there!" Charlotte insisted.

Victoria gave Owen an uncertain look, which he was sure had to do with leaving the Sugar Plum in the care of two people she doubted she could trust.

Unable to say anything in front of Britney and Charlotte, Owen took Victoria's hand and gave it a squeeze. He didn't figure there was too much mischief the two women could get into and still cover their posts at the inn. And if they did commit a crime while he and Victoria were out, it would give him one more opportunity to gather evidence against them.

So he was all for leaving. Besides, he wanted to spend some time with Victoria watching their daughter in the parade.

The two of them stood on the crowded porch and watched the parade go by. When the Sunday school float came into view, Victoria pulled her camera from her jacket pocket and quickly snapped a couple of pictures of Paige before waving to her daughter. Owen, caught up in the festivities, put his fingers in his mouth and let loose a wolf whistle, startling both Paige and Victoria, who quickly recovered from their surprise and laughed.

As the float took the corner at the end of the block, Owen grabbed Victoria's hand again and pulled her toward the stairs. "Come on." He leaned close to her ear to be heard over the din of the crowd. "They'll end up at the park. We can fetch Paige there."

Victoria nodded and they made their way through the green-faced crowd.

They reached the park, where the high school band had already set up and was playing near the gazebo. A sound system had been erected from the prominent spot, for the announcement of the winning parade entries. There would be more contests and events throughout the day.

Owen and Victoria skirted the gazebo and found

the place where the floats were leaving off their riders. Soon Paige's float arrived, and Paige stood on the edge of the high platform, looking nervous about jumping down.

"May I help you?" Owen reached his hands up toward Paige.

She nodded happily and jumped into his waiting arms. For a second she hugged him tight. "Thank you!" she chirped before tossing herself at her mother.

Owen watched them embrace and felt his chest swell with emotion. The mother and daughter made such a pretty picture, with Paige in her lovely green dress and Victoria's cheeks glowing red from the cold. He took a step back and watched the two of them together, as Paige happily recounted her adventure and Victoria listened.

With no one else to talk to, he found himself carrying on a silent conversation with God. *Can You help me earn Victoria's trust, Lord? Can You help me win back her heart? If You see fit to give me this family, I promise I'll love them forever and do everything I can to keep them safe.*

Victoria looked up at him and smiled. "Paige wants to listen for the winners of the float contest."

"I'm sure you have time. There can't be many customers at the Sugar Plum—everyone is here."

Indeed, the people who had filled the streets now crammed the park so full they could hardly get through the crowd to the grandstand. Burke Hennessy, the longtime chair of the parade committee, was already at the microphone, making witty remarks to the crowd between the band's song sets. When the band played a festive number, Burke motioned to his wife, Christina, who joined him on the gazebo and danced a couple of turns before the song ended.

The crowd clapped and cheered and Burke, flush-faced, grabbed the microphone again. "Do we have the results of the parade contest? I hate to keep the good people of Fitzgerald Bay waiting."

The judging panel, which sat on an elevated booth facing the parade route, turned and shook their heads. They appeared to be caught up in deliberation.

Burke spoke into the microphone again. "Like I said, I hate to keep the good people of Fitzgerald Bay waiting. That's why I'd like to take this opportunity to apologize to everyone for the poor job our local police department has done investigating the awful murder of Olivia Henry."

The crowd seemed to suck in its breath, and there was no sound but the wind and a metallic wail as a band member collapsed a trombone en route to its case. Owen felt his heart nearly stop. He knew people around town had been whispering similar words, but to hear them proclaimed from a microphone was another thing entirely.

Burke's dyed-blond comb-over fluttered in the wind as he faced the people gathered below him. "It's not fair to all of you to have to live with uncertainty. We know Charles Fitzgerald was a lonely man. We know Olivia Henry was a lovely girl. We know what his motives were." Burke's beady eyes scanned the crowd.

No one protested. No one spoke in the Fitzgeralds' defense.

"People of Fitzgerald Bay, *Charles Fitzgerald is the prime suspect in the murder of Olivia Henry!* So why hasn't he been arrested for his crimes?"

Silence.

"I come before you today to say *it's time!* It's time for no more waiting! It's time for answers! It's time for Charles Fitzgerald to face a full investigation. It's time, Fitzgerald Bay, time for justice and answers and peace!"

He'd gotten the crowd worked up into a fervor, all right. The people appeared to be on the verge of cheering.

Burke must have sensed it, too, because he gripped the microphone harder. "It's time for a new era, Fitzgerald Bay. That's why today, I am privileged to announce to you, that the reign of secrets of the Fitzgeralds clan is about to come to an end. I have thrown my hat in the mayoral race, and ask for your vote for me, Burke Hennessy, for mayor of Fitzgerald Bay!"

He gave a little jump and a whoop at the end, and the baited crowd jumped and whooped with him. The cheer erupted all around them, and Owen shook his head. He glanced around for his family members, but the crowd was so large, he couldn't spot any of them.

He agreed it was time the people of Fitzgerald Bay got some answers. But he was equally convinced Burke Hennessy wasn't the man to give them those answers.

Victoria held tightly to Paige's hand as they followed Owen back to the outskirts of the crowd, where the din of cheering wasn't quite so loud, nor the crush of people as dense. She gave him a sympathetic look and tugged on his hand. "It's mostly out-of-town people in the crowd," she pointed out. "They don't know your brother."

But Owen didn't look reassured. He'd already told her he couldn't prove Charles was innocent.

Fortunately, the panel of judges burst through the crowd with a fat envelope, and the cheering dimmed enough for Burke to begin announcing the winners of the various categories in the parade. The silence around her hummed with expectancy and murmurs, as people began whispering about Burke's candidacy and speech.

Victoria's ears pricked up, and she felt Paige's small hand tug on her own. When she looked down, her daughter's face was white and her eyes round with fear. "Mommy—the humming," Paige whispered, and nodded backward toward the crowd behind them.

Listening carefully, Victoria picked up the sound,

and her head supplied the words to go with it. She knew that song. "The Wreck of the Edmund Fitzgerald."

She grabbed Owen's hand and gave it a jerk. "Humming," she mouthed, and tipped her head toward the sound.

Owen must have seen the fear on her face. His eyes narrowed as they scanned the thinning crowd, and he took a couple of steps backward, scenting out the source of the song.

Burke announced the third-place band, and a cheer covered the song, but Victoria caught the humming notes again as the cheering stilled, and followed Owen back through the crowd.

"There." She squeezed Owen's hand and pointed to a man ten feet behind them, his green-painted face turned mostly away from them.

"Mommy." Paige pulled on her other hand and whispered urgently. "There he is—the man who robbed the safe!"

Owen bent down and caught the last of Paige's words, then dropped Victoria's hand and darted toward the broad-shouldered figure. The crowd blocked his way and he sidestepped through the filtering people, making two more strides toward the humming man before the green face glanced back. The man saw him coming and fled.

TWELVE

Victoria scooped Paige up into her arms before the girl could go tearing off after Owen.

"We've got to catch him!" Paige fought to get her feet on the ground.

"Paige, no." Victoria held her tightly and watched as Owen sprinted after the man. "Let the detective catch him. This isn't a game."

"But, Mom, he's getting away."

Victoria let out a long breath as she watched Owen's vain scramble after the retreating man, whose head start and green face paint made him blend in so easily with the crowd. "Let's hurry, then." She held Paige's hand tightly and they trotted off in the direction Owen had run.

She found him stomping on the sidewalk near the parade route, checking every doorway and the head of every alley, a disgusted expression on his face.

"Did you get a good look at him?" She hoped they might at least have picked up a clue.

"He had a green face and a black jacket, just like

hundreds of other folks here today. He could be standing right in front of me right now and I wouldn't be able to tell you if it was him."

"I'd recognize him if I saw him again," Paige declared.

"I know, Paige," Victoria assured her daughter before turning to Owen. "Do you want to retrace your steps and look for a footprint?"

"In this crowd?" Owen shook his head. "Let's head back to the Sugar Plum. The crowd at the park is already thinning. They're going to want lunch soon."

Indeed, as they neared the Sugar Plum, Victoria could see the café was already hopping with customers. She picked up her pace and Paige hurried along beside her.

"I'll change out of my dress and come help you."

Victoria's heart crushed. Her little girl was always helping. And yet, who was she to turn down an extra set of hands? Paige had already proved to be capable of busing tables—and they'd need busing, if the growing line to the counter was any indication.

"I'll help, too," Owen insisted as they ducked around to the kitchen entrance.

They stepped inside and Victoria immediately recoiled at the sight of a green-painted face and black jacket hard at work scooping steaming bowls of chowder from the warming vats she'd left on low for their noon soup special.

Britney poked her head in as the male handed off

a tray of bowls. "Clint said he'd help out. I hope you don't mind—Charlotte and I were having trouble keeping up. I made him wash his hands."

Victoria swallowed back her protests. "I appreciate the help," she called after Britney as the girl hurried away to the waiting customers. Then she exchanged looks with Owen, who looked the youth up and down, before leaning close to her ear and whispering.

"He's dressed like the man I chased. He could have made it here ahead of us."

"I could ask Britney how long he's been here," Victoria offered. "But Paige already said he didn't do it."

"And it looks like you could use his help," Owen agreed.

Victoria nodded and smiled at Clint as he glanced back at them. "Thank you for your help. I'll wash my hands and get to work."

Paige retreated upstairs to change her dress, and Owen joined Victoria at the sink.

The noon crowd didn't thin until after two o'clock. Victoria had to nearly force Paige to take a break at noon and have some lunch, or the little girl would have kept busing tables straight through mealtime.

When she mentioned as much to Owen, he laughed. "And when did *you* take a lunch break?" He shook his head and carried off more bowls of steaming soup. "Like mother, like daughter."

As she watched him go, it didn't escape Victoria's notice that Owen hadn't stopped for lunch, either. So perhaps Paige had inherited her hardworking tendency from both sides of the family.

As Victoria was prepping the food for the evening buffet, Charlotte stuck her head in the kitchen. "We have a couple here looking for a room."

Victoria's eyes widened. She'd booked most of the rooms ahead of the weekend and taken down the vacancy sign because there was only one room left, and it wasn't ready to receive visitors. She stepped to the podium to talk to the couple.

And older man had his arm slung around his wife's waist. "We didn't make reservations because we thought we'd be headed home. But the weather report is calling for another blizzard, so Madge thought maybe, if you had a room for the night…"

Victoria nodded. She didn't want to turn the elderly pair away, especially not with a storm moving in. "I have one more room, but right now the flowers that sit on my porch during the summer are overwintering there. If you'll give me half an hour I can have the room ready."

The man looked relieved. "We'll have the cookie-and-coffee special while we wait."

Charlotte rang up the purchase, and Victoria headed for the stairs.

Owen followed her. "I'll help you with the plants."

She didn't argue. The huge hanging baskets that encircled the wide porch during the summer months were plenty heavy, and there were eight large ones, plus several more pots that sat on the porch floor during the mild months. It would take her half an hour just to move the plants, and then she'd have to make up the room. "I appreciate your help," she told Owen sincerely as they headed down the hall to the far room, whose many wide windows overlooked the side and back yards.

"Chilly up here," Owen commented.

Victoria had felt the temperature dip as they climbed the stairs. "I hope it's not a problem with the furnace." She pulled out her keys and unlocked the seldom-used room.

"No!" She gasped as she took in the extent of the mess.

Broken windows greeted her, the curtains torn, plants toppled and trampled, dirt everywhere, even smeared in muddy streaks across the wallpaper. Cold air blasted in on the wind, and the once-green leaves of the plants had taken on a decidedly blackened hue.

"It's ruined. The whole room." She gasped for her breath, and didn't fight Owen when he pulled her against his shoulder, blocking her eyes from the horrible scene. "How? Who?"

"We'll find them."

"They're long gone. The temperature has been above freezing since midmorning, but the plants have frostbite. That means whoever did this came in the night." She shuddered at the thought that, while she and Paige and the other guests had been quietly sleeping, someone had been just on the other side of the wall, destroying the lovely plants, and the room.

"Those muddy smears on the walls are full of fin-gerprints. We'll catch them this time."

Victoria clung to his shoulders and choked back a sob.

"It's going to be okay." Owen rubbed her back, soothing her while she fought the fury and helpless-ness that assaulted her every time she looked at the room.

Pushing away from the comfort of his embrace, Victoria wiped back her tears and caught a glimpse of herself in the broken mirror above the dresser on the opposite wall. Her cheeks were already blotchy from crying, and her face was tear-streaked. "I need to tell that couple that I don't have a room for them after all." She sniffled back another sob and tried to compose herself.

"Mommy?" Paige's voice carried down the hall.

"I'll get her." Owen turned to meet Paige.

"Hurry—don't let her see." Victoria bit back an-other gulp of fear. "I don't want her to be frightened. Her bedroom is right next to this one."

Owen trotted down the hall to meet Paige. He didn't want the girl to see her mother's tear-streaked face. Knowing Paige, she'd insist on finding out exactly why her mother had been crying. "Paige!" He threw on a smile and quickly thought of a way to keep Paige away while they cleaned up the mess. "Remember how my dad gave you that gift certificate to the Reading Nook last week?"

"Yes." Her eyes twinkled.

"You've done such a good job helping your mom today, how about if we go over to the Reading Nook and get you another gift certificate?"

"Really?" She took the bend in the hall that led to the small apartment she and Victoria shared. "I'll get my jacket."

Relieved that his ruse had worked, Owen ducked inside the apartment after Paige and made a cursory sweep of the space to be sure that nothing in their private quarters had been disturbed.

No broken glass. No smears of mud. They were safe—for now.

Paige placed one trusting hand in his. "Ready?"

He smiled down in wonder at the little face that looked so much like his at that age. "Let's go."

Owen left Paige in the care of his sister Fiona, who sent her straight to the middle-grade shelves to browse. He quickly handed over cash for a gift certificate and explained the situation, leaving out the detail, of course, that Paige was his daughter. Fiona, a loving mother, was quick to agree to watch Paige.

His sister and the rest of his extended family would soon learn there was another Fitzgerald among them. But how would they take the news?

Rushing back down the block to the Sugar Plum,

Owen arrived just as Victoria, her face washed clean of her tears, explained the situation to the waiting couple.

"I'm afraid there's a broken window, and some plants have toppled over." She disguised a sniffle as a hiccup, shaking her head with regret. "I won't be able to have the room ready for you after all."

The couple was very understanding, but they got on their way in a hurry to get home before the storm hit.

Owen could see it broke Victoria's heart to turn them away, but he knew the storm was still a ways off, and the couple would have plenty of time to make it home before the weather got bad. In the meantime, he didn't want her messing with the room. It was a crime scene.

He explained as much to her as they ducked back into the kitchen. "I'll call over to the station and get a crew to check it out. We'll have to record the finger-prints and look for any other clues before the mess gets cleaned up."

"But the windows—"

"I'll board them over. Do you have any more boards?"

"I have the ones from the window that was replaced in the back dining room." A carpenter had been over to fix the window earlier that week. "But they won't be enough for the whole suite. The entire west wall is windows."

Owen shushed her protests. "I'll come up with the wood. I don't even want you to go up there again. You've got your hands full down here."

Victoria looked as though she'd like to argue with him, but he knew there was little she could say against his plan. She nodded resignedly. "You're right. I'll get the corned beef brisket cooking."

While Victoria headed off to the kitchen, Owen hurried up the stairs and pulled out his phone. He asked the police dispatcher to send his sister Keira and her partner, Nick Delfino, over to investigate. Then he eyeballed the size of the wall-length shattered windows and called his father.

"Do you still have those sheets of plywood in your garage?" he asked his dad, quickly obtaining permission to borrow them. He thanked his father, but before he closed the call, Aiden Fitzgerald cleared his throat.

"Owen?"

"Yes, Dad?"

"I want you to watch the six o'clock local news. I'll talk to you later. Bye."

Before Owen could ask his father for more information about his cryptic request, their call had ended. Wondering what that was all about, he shoved his phone back into his pocket and fished out the keys to his Ford Raptor pickup. He'd arrived at the Sugar Plum on foot, but he'd need the truck bed to haul the plywood sheets to board over the windows.

When he returned, Keira and Nick were gathering fingerprints and photographing the scene.

"Mind if I board over the windows?"

"Please." His little sister shivered. "We did them first so you could get the wind blocked. It's cold in here and that storm is coming in fast."

Owen glowered at the sky as he set the first sheet of wood in place. Yup, they'd get plenty of snow. Victoria probably wouldn't have a big crowd for supper after all. He knew she'd be disappointed by the lost revenue, but at the same time, the woman had put in a full day already. She could use a bit of a break.

Too bad she now had the added expense of fixing the damaged room, and a slow night would mean less income to cover the expense.

"Any idea who might have done this?" Owen asked Keira and Nick as they worked.

"Somebody who wasn't worried about their fingerprints being collected," Nick observed.

Owen paused on his way back out to the hallway for another sheet of plywood. "What do you mean?"

"I've taken at least fifteen clear prints. Nobody would be stupid enough to leave behind that much personal evidence unless they had reason to believe it wouldn't be traced to them."

Nick's words struck an ominous note.

Owen looked around the room, the fingerprints he'd earlier viewed with hope now taunting him from every wall.

* * *

Victoria had filled the buffet servers nearly to overflowing and stood back, waiting for the crowd to arrive.

A smatter of sleetlike snow pellets slammed against the windows, thrown by a furious wind. She wanted to cry. After all her work, would any customers brave the storm to eat?

Charlotte looked up from another phone call and crossed another name off their list. "Another cancellation." She clucked her tongue. "No one wants to come out in the storm."

Britney stepped out from the kitchen. "Clint was saying maybe I should head home. This storm is getting bad, and my folks live outside of town."

Victoria checked her watch. It was almost six, and the few customers who'd braved the weather wouldn't be any trouble for her to handle by herself. "Good idea. How about if I send home dinner for your family? I've got plenty."

"Sure." Britney and Clint exchanged glances. "Thank you."

"I'm more than happy to do it. I appreciate all your help today. In fact—" She paused at the front podium on her way to the kitchen and pulled out a form from a file. "Clint, if you can fill this out, I'll make sure you get paid for your work today."

The young man looked surprised, but pleased. "Thanks. I could use the money."

Unsure whether she could trust the pair or not, Victoria pulled out a large ceramic pan and heaped a feast inside. Sealing the lid on top, she handed it to Britney and apologized. "Sorry I didn't use a disposable pan. I'm afraid this meal is too juicy for a to-go box."

"No problem. Thanks again!" Britney and Clint tromped out the back door, and Victoria watched them leave. Were the two of them behind the rash of break-ins? *Had* Britney's father been involved with her father's car wreck ten years before? Victoria figured, if nothing else, she and Owen might use fetching the pan as an excuse to travel out to the Murtagh place and see what kind of clues they might turn up.

But in the meantime, she needed to fetch her daughter from the Reading Nook.

Owen adjusted the volume on the small television set in Victoria's kitchen. His father had told him to watch the evening news. Other than a weather report, and maybe a replay of Hennessy's speech at the park that day, Owen wasn't sure what his father thought was so important for him to see. But he tuned in just the same.

As the anchorman cut to commercials, Victoria and Paige blew in the back door, stomping snow from their shoes as they entered.

"Any more customers?" Victoria asked quietly.

"Charlotte's ringing up the last of them, and then she asked about heading home."

Victoria took the news in stride. She'd likely anticipated as much. "I'll let her know she can leave."

While Victoria stepped up front, Paige showed off her new books to Owen. Then the commercials ended and the news coverage showed the scene from the park earlier that day.

"Hoping to catch another glimpse of our humming stranger?" Victoria asked as she returned to the room, stepping close behind him to watch the footage on the small screen.

"That's a good idea. I actually tuned in because my father told me I needed to watch—" His words dropped off as a panoramic shot of the crowd drew his attention. He caught a glimpse of the three of them together, looking just like any other happy family enjoying the festival. Rather than admire the pleasant picture they made together, he forced himself to scour the crowd behind them.

"There." He pointed to a man at the same moment Victoria's finger flew forward, identifying the same figure. They caught just a glimpse of him before the footage switched back to the scene at the gazebo.

"Did you see enough to identify him?" Owen asked, his hope dimming.

"Not with all that green face paint on. I couldn't even rule out Clint."

She had a good point. Owen listened with half an

ear to Burke's speech, which he would have much rather quickly forgotten. As the cheering crowd faded out, the newscaster announced a rebuttal from the opposition.

"This must be what my father wanted me to watch for." He turned the volume up a notch as his grandfather Ian Fitzgerald appeared on the screen, flanked on each side by sons Aiden and Mickey. Owen's uncle Mickey wore his chief firefighter's dress uniform, and Aiden, too, had on his finest navy police uniform jacket complete with all his medals.

They certainly made an impressive picture, though Owen thought his grandfather was showing his age— undoubtedly because the current situation had been weighing on him.

Still, the mayor of Fitzgerald Bay spoke with a firm and steady voice. "We need to set the record straight. There has been no cover-up by the police, as some have suggested. Charles Fitzgerald is innocent of any crime. If anyone has evidence relating to the death of Olivia Henry, we encourage them to come forward. Until then, I and my family remain confident that Charles Fitzgerald, a respected physician who has selflessly given his time and energy to the people of our community, is in no way connected to the murder."

There was no cheering crowd to follow the announcement, only the grim expressions of the news anchors as they repeated the request for anyone with information about Olivia's murder to come forward.

Owen stared at the television screen even after the program was replaced by a commercial for Connolly's Catch Seafood Store and Restaurant, the local restaurant owned by his Aunt Vanessa and Uncle Joe. After a few more commercials the weather report came on, calling for snow throughout most of the evening, tapering off by eleven o'clock. Sunday would start out crisp, but the sun was supposed to come out and warm things up, melting away much of the snow.

The sigh behind his shoulder told him Victoria felt discouraged by the prospect of a snow-filled evening. "I suppose instead of cooking the rest of these briskets, I should put them back in the freezer. Don't be surprised if I have a special on Reuben sandwiches every day for the next several months."

"Hank Monroe will love that. Reubens are his favorite."

Victoria grumbled as she disappeared into the walk-in fridge. When she didn't come back out, Owen stuck his head in, and found her transferring several large vacuum-packed bags of meat through a second door in the back of the fridge, which he discovered led to the freezer.

"It's like a hidden room back here." He observed the frozen boxes and crates of meats, vegetables and hash browns.

"My secret ice cave." Victoria chuckled. "When I worked here during high school, sometimes I'd hide back here."

Her revelation surprised Owen. "Hide? From your manager?"

"No." She looked embarrassed. "Just if someone came by who I didn't want to see."

"Who?"

Victoria sighed. "Hank Monroe. He used to come by a lot, even when you and I had started dating. I guess I was supposed to be flattered by the attention, but he had a way of making nasty comments—not outright, you know. Friendly on the surface, but with sharp teeth under them." She shoved another package of beef high onto a freezer shelf.

"He never did stop spreading the rumors about you, did he?" Owen hauled the last two bags of meat to the back freezer.

"Never did." She shook her head. "If I could figure out how to make him stop, I would." She headed for the door that led back into the kitchen. "I should check on Paige."

Owen followed her back into the kitchen, where Paige had pulled out a game she'd bought with her Reading Nook gift certificate. With few customers to tend to, he and Victoria sat down and played the game with Paige, eventually stopping to help themselves to the delicious buffet.

To his surprise, Victoria never asked him to leave.

Perhaps she figured he'd object on account of the weather, although his townhome wasn't that many blocks away, and he had his truck. He could have made it home with no problem.

To his delight, Victoria and her daughter relaxed, and seemed to thoroughly enjoy spending time with him. As the evening wore on, he found himself wishing it could last forever.

The image of the three of them in the park together flashed through his mind. They'd looked something like a family. Owen fought against the yearning in his heart. He could list a dozen reasons why he'd be foolish to marry Victoria. But every time she smiled at him, all those reasons faded away.

All too soon, Victoria announced to Paige, "It's getting close to bedtime. We've got church tomorrow, so you need to take a bath."

"I can watch the restaurant," Owen assured the two of them quickly. The guests at the inn had already eaten and retired to their rooms, so Owen didn't figure he'd have his hands very full.

"Thanks." Victoria headed for the stairs. "Give me a holler if the crowd gets too big for you." They both laughed. Far short of a crowd, they'd seen a mere handful of customers since Charlotte had left.

When Victoria came back downstairs half an hour later, Owen had already started cleaning the kitchen. He'd hoped for some time alone to discuss the day's events with Victoria, and to try to sort out if she could make any meaning of them. She reluctantly agreed to let him wash dishes while she locked up and ran the day's report.

"Normally I'd be pleased by today's total," she remarked on her way to the safe with the bank bag a bit later. "But I'm sure the windows are going to cost more than I made today."

Owen dried off his hands and was at her side by the time she rose from locking the safe.

He extended his arms toward her, unsure how close she'd let him get, and was surprised when she leaned her head on his shoulder and returned his embrace. His arms tightened around her protectively, and he wished he could hold her forever and guard her from whoever was causing her trouble. He wanted to reassure her that things were going to be fine, but he couldn't lie to her. Even more than her state of mind, he was worried for her safety. "You can't keep going like this. These attacks aren't going away."

"But the fingerprints—you said they would prove whoever did this. It's going to end."

"If we can match the prints to someone in the system." Owen paused, unsure how much of Nick's grim prognosis he should share. He didn't want to discourage Victoria, but at the same time, he didn't feel the Sugar Plum was a safe place. "But until then, I'm not convinced it's safe for you and Paige to continue staying here. I have plenty of room at my place—"

"What?" Victoria jerked her head away from him,

glaring directly into his eyes. "You agreed not to take Paige overnight until she's had a chance to get to know you."

Owen leaned closer, shaking his head. "That's not what I mean. I don't think it's safe for either of you here." He couldn't shake the image of the three of them as a family. Maybe he was foolish for hoping they could be one, but he wanted to try. "Paige is our daughter. I'd like to raise her together."

"What are you saying?"

"You used to love me. I know you're upset right now, and everything is *complicated*—" He used the same words she had used to sum up the situation. "But I care about what happens to you and Paige. I want to protect you. I can't do that with you living here."

"You want us to move in with you? Owen, I couldn't—"

"I was thinking more along the lines of getting married."

"Are you insane?" She pulled out of his arms.

He let her go. Her automatic refusal crushed his heart. Maybe it *was* a crazy idea after all.

Victoria continued. "It's nothing personal. Paige told me she doesn't want to move. We moved all the time before we came here—for a better place, for lower rent, we were always moving. We came here to stay." She let out a frustrated-sounding breath.

Victoria shook her head. "Your family hates me. They would never approve."

Owen didn't argue with her. Though he wasn't certain his family *hated* her, he knew they weren't particularly keen on the daughter of the man they all believed had killed their cousin. Though he knew the truth, he didn't know how he could ever prove to them that Stanley Evans hadn't caused Patrick's death—that in fact, Victoria's father had been just as much a victim of a violent crime that night as their cousin had been.

As he watched Victoria walk away, he realized she was right. A lot of things had happened in the past ten years, and no matter how strong his feelings were for her now, he didn't see how they could ever get past that.

THIRTEEN

Owen didn't realize until after he sat down at church the next morning that Victoria and Paige were situated directly in his line of sight as he faced the preacher. Since the service was getting started, he could hardly get up and move elsewhere. Besides, though he didn't want them to feel he was spying on them, it was interesting to watch the pair as Victoria helped Paige bow her head to pray, and opened their Bibles to follow along with the scripture reading together.

Owen listened intently to the pastor's message. Pastor Larch talked about worry, and how worrying drove people away from God. Owen certainly understood the truth of that statement.

The pastor went on to explain that, by taking their worries to God in prayer instead of fretting over them, they could move closer to God *and* have their prayers answered.

The explanation was so simple, Owen wondered why it had never occurred to him before. Could God really handle all the problems in his life, if he simply prayed about them instead of worrying over them? Though it seemed far too simplistic to work, Owen had tried everything else he could think of.

As the pastor called for a time of prayer, Owen bent his head and prayed for everything: the situation at the Sugar Plum, his feelings for Paige and Victoria, and all the messy jumble of the past, including Patrick's death and the unsolved mystery of who had caused the accident.

When he raised his head again, he felt a greater sense of peace.

And he got a happy surprise when Paige gave him a hug after the service. "What's that for?" he asked, touched by her gesture.

Paige shrugged. "You're nice," she declared simply, and scampered away to her blushing mother.

Waving goodbye, Owen headed home to dress for work. His father expected him at the police station when his shift began at two. And Owen realized that would be the best place for him. He needed to get to work processing the evidence Keira and Nick had gathered. Because ultimately, the only way he was going to keep Victoria and Paige safe was by catching whoever was behind the break-ins.

Arriving plenty early for his shift, Owen was surprised to find Keira already at work on the evidence. His little sister scowled at the computer screen and punched a few more buttons.

"You're here early."

"So are you." More scowling.

"Computer disagreeing with you?"

"Yes. Before you give me any flak about being the rookie, I want you to try this for yourself." Keira hopped out of her chair and motioned for him to take a turn at the machine.

"What is it?"

"I entered the fingerprints we took from the walls at the Sugar Plum yesterday. They're coming up with a perfect match on the internal system."

"That means they belong to a local person whose fingerprints are already in the system. That's good news. We finally have our perp. So, why are you scowling?"

"Click to see the match."

Owen hit the button.

File not found.

"What?" Owen clicked the button again. "That can't be right."

"I've tried going at it ten different ways, last night and again this afternoon. The computer recognizes that the fingerprints belong to someone in the internal system, but it can't find the file."

"Why not?"

Keira blew out a long breath. "It's gone."

While the bright sun melted the fresh snow, a steady stream of customers filled the Sugar Plum. To Victoria's immense relief, many of them were interested in the corned beef and cabbage special they'd missed out on the day before. Business slowed midafternoon just long enough for Victoria to spend time with Paige practicing her latest voice-lesson songs at the dining room piano.

She was just cleaning up from the supper crowd when the door bells jangled.

Owen Fitzgerald gave her a sheepish look, almost as though he feared she might throw him out.

Her heart plummeted, and she felt guilty about how she'd handled their conversation the evening before. There would have been a time when she'd have been over the moon if Owen had proposed to her, but she was nearly certain, given their circumstances, that such a move would only bring more pain to her, to Owen and, even more so, to Paige. And from the cautious way Owen had popped the question, she was nearly certain he knew it, too. In fact, she realized later, part of the reason she'd refused him so sharply was because his proposal had sounded more like a plan to solve their safety issue and not a declaration of love.

Still, she needed to hear what he'd stopped by to say, and waved him back to the kitchen, where Paige sat at the counter engrossed in one of the books she'd picked out the day before. Rather than say what she needed to in front of Paige, she pulled Owen into the walk-in fridge.

He cleared his throat as the door shut behind them. "We ran the fingerprints from yesterday's crime scene."

"Did you find anything?"

The expression on Owen's face was part discouraged, part distressed. "Sort of. The computer identified the prints as being a perfect match with a set in our internal system."

"Internal system?" Victoria repeated. "What's that?"

"It's the collection of all the fingerprints that have been taken locally—from anyone we've booked here in Fitzgerald Bay, anyone who's applied for a job with us or any kids who've gone through the local school system."

"So the crime was committed by a local person." Victoria absorbed the news and braced herself for the revelation she felt hanging between them. "Okay, who was it?"

The apology in Owen's eyes sent her heart rate rocketing.

"Just tell me." She braced herself. Was it someone she knew? Someone she trusted?

"We don't know. The file is missing."

"What? I thought you said it was a perfect match."

"It *is*. The fingerprints belong to someone in the FBPD system. The computer has retained the initial search capacity on the file, but the file itself is gone."

"Gone? Gone where?"

Owen placed his steady hands on her shoulders,

which Victoria realized were shaking. She forced herself to stop trembling and to look into his eyes.

"When Nick and Keira took the prints, they wondered why anyone would be foolish enough to leave such clear evidence behind. The only answer we can devise is that whoever was behind this crime had already removed their file from the system. They left their fingerprints because they knew they couldn't be traced back to them. Ultimately, whoever did this thinks they're above the law."

His words settled over her like the chill of the fridge.

She swallowed back a lump of fear and forced her teeth to stop chattering. "They're not afraid of being caught?"

She had hardly spoken when the radio buzzed on Owen's belt. "I need to get back to work," he murmured, before quickly responding to the call.

Victoria nodded and left him to the privacy of the walk-in fridge. Paige looked up from her reading and smiled. "You and Owen like to go in the refrigerator together."

Though Paige's words sounded like an innocent observation, Victoria couldn't help blushing, and struggled to think of a response.

Fortunately, Owen emerged from the fridge a second later, distracting Paige.

"I need to get back to work. All those tourists in town…" He threw his hands up in the air and left his sentence unfinished, retreating with a wave. "I'll see you ladies later."

Paige waved back until the front door bells jangled after Owen. Then the girl giggled. "He's fun."

"Yes." Victoria qualified her statement. "He certainly makes life interesting, doesn't he?"

Victoria spent the next week mulling over her discussion with Owen. Beyond the unresolved issue of how to keep Paige safe, she now found herself distracted by the growing feelings she had for him and her thoughts about his tempting, though crazy, marriage proposal.

Over and over again, she told herself nothing good could possibly come from it. Ten years before, the Fitzgeralds had given her the strong impression that they felt she was not good enough for one of them. They were a close-knit family, and zealously protected their own. They saw her as a threat. Given the rumors Hank had spread about her, they probably feared she'd lead Owen astray.

Though she'd tried everything she could think of to win their favor—baking them pies, cupcakes, turnovers and dozens of cinnamon rolls, none of them had ever expressed anything more than a cursory thankyou, coupled at times with a wary look, as though they suspected she had some underlying treacherous motive.

That was *before* the wreck involving her father and

Patrick. Whatever the white paint on her father's truck meant, neither she nor Owen had found the source of it, nor likely would they. So it stood to reason that the Fitzgeralds would probably scorn her still, and that much more so for what they believed her father had done to their cousin. Despite the lack of alcohol in his system.

Add to that all the horrible rumors Hank Monroe had spread since then, which it seemed everyone in town except Owen believed, and she knew she had no reason to even *think* about Owen Fitzgerald. There was only heartache down that road.

Too bad she couldn't stop thinking about what it might feel like to kiss him again.

By Saturday she was in a funk, partly because she saw no way out of the situation, partly because she knew Owen would eventually want to formalize the joint custody arrangement, whatever his assurances in the refrigerator had been, and partly because the weather was still overcast and dreary, and she'd almost forgotten what it felt like to stand in the sun.

Owen stopped by as the trickle of lunch customers began to disperse, and Victoria bused the tables in the empty back dining room. His face held a mischievous smile. "Does Paige have plans for this afternoon?"

She would have liked to deny it, but Victoria had to admit, "She doesn't."

His smile brightened. "Charles is taking his twins

to the matinee. It's that new animated movie all the youngsters have been waiting for."

Victoria knew exactly which movie Owen was talking about. Paige had been talking about it, too, but since her daughter knew they were always too busy to go to the movies, Paige hadn't even asked to go.

She felt a wistful longing take hold of her heart. Paige would love to go to the film. "What time?"

"We'd need to leave in half an hour or less." He looked at her expectantly.

Victoria didn't know what to say. "Are you asking for my permission?"

"I guess so."

"She'd be delighted to go."

"So, you'll let her?"

"Is it up to me?" Victoria dropped a few plates into the waiting gray tub with a bit of an extra clonk.

"You're her mother."

Victoria heaved the heavy tub onto the table and bit back a surprising well of emotion, unsure why their conversation affected her so much. Was it because she'd love to take her daughter to the movies herself, but she never had the time? Or was it because, deep down, she didn't feel Owen should have to ask her permission to take Paige anywhere?

"You're her father. If you want to take her anywhere, it's enough for you to just let me know where you'll be and when you'll be back. I trust your judgment."

Owen's face brightened. "So it's okay?"

"It's more than okay, Owen. I think it's great. Paige will love going to the movies with you. Let me find her." Victoria spun around in time to see Paige entering the room.

"Did you just say movies?" Paige's bright-eyed expression looked nearly the same as Owen's.

Victoria swallowed back a lump in her throat. She couldn't speak, but fortunately Owen jumped in, revealing the plan to take Paige to see the movie with Charles and the twins.

Paige was so excited, she didn't even seem to mind that the twins were several years younger than she was. She ran for the stairs. "Let me get my jacket!"

Owen took a step after her, but Victoria snagged his jacket and pulled him back. "Are you planning to tell her?"

"Not without you. I thought maybe after the movie, we could come back here for supper. And then, if you get a break…" Owen shrugged, his expression hopeful.

"Okay." Victoria tried to breathe evenly in spite of the rising tide of emotions she felt. So far, Owen had been kind about the situation—kinder than she'd expected him to be. But she fought against the rising sense of panic from knowing that he would eventually take Paige from her for longer than a movie matinee.

Paige fairly flew down the stairs and waved her cell phone at her mother. "I'm ready!" Owen took her hand, and with another backward wave, they were out the door.

As she cleaned the kitchen and prepared for the evening crowd, Victoria tried to tell herself not to be jealous of Owen. Yes, Paige was thrilled to go to the movies with him. He deserved to spend time with his daughter as much as she did. But she wished her little girl would have at least paused to hug her goodbye.

The dinner hour approached, and with each jangle of the bells on the door, Victoria found herself looking up, expecting to see Owen and Paige, and hoping for a hug from her daughter.

Instead, customers kept arriving—not that she was about to complain. When the door clattered open again and a broad-shouldered silhouette appeared in her peripheral vision, Victoria turned toward the door with a smile, expecting a hug from Paige any moment.

Hank Monroe entered, stomping his boots on the welcome mat.

"What can I get for you today?" Victoria asked.

"Can we talk?"

With a glance at the contented customers in the dining room, Victoria decided she could spare a moment, especially since Charlotte had arrived and was already chatting up some newcomers in the back dining room.

"Sure." Victoria led him closer to the glass display case, out of the way of entering patrons. "What's up?"

"I did a little checking on those muddy fingerprints

from your break-in last week. They belong to someone here in town."

Since she already knew that much, Victoria wondered what Hank was getting at. "Do you know who?"

"Owen."

Victoria recoiled in shock, stepping backward until she came up against the pastry case. "Are you certain?"

Hank scowled. "I can't be certain without printing him again. But you know how it is with those Fitzgeralds. They're covering for Charles. They'll cover for Owen, too. I have no doubt that's why the prints mysteriously disappeared. That's why I came to you first. You and Owen get along all right, don't you?"

Victoria nodded.

"I need you to gather his fingerprints and pass them along to me. I'll do the rest."

Victoria sucked in a slow breath and tried to think. "But why would Owen do this?"

"To get back at you. Your dad killed his cousin, remember? Maybe he doesn't want you in town anymore."

Victoria tried to wrap her mind around what Hank was saying, but it didn't make any sense. The fingerprints couldn't belong to Owen. What was Hank up to?

"I want to help you catch him." Hank's features softened. "All I need you to do is have Owen leave his fingerprints on something—a drinking glass, a door, anything, as long as you get a decent set of clear prints. Then call me right away. I'll do the rest."

"But I—"

The hand on her shoulder squeezed uncomfortably tight. "You want it to end, don't you?"

"Of course I do. But—"

There was no way Owen was guilty of anything.

"As soon as Owen's in jail, I guarantee, all your troubles will be over." He smiled a charming smile and sealed it with a wink.

Before Victoria could respond, Paige burst through the door with a flurry of sound, and Hank's hand flew from her shoulder.

"Mommy!"

"Paige!" Victoria scooped her little girl up gratefully. "Did you have a good time?"

"It was the best! I got popcorn and chocolate and soda—"

"Soda?"

"Clear soda." Owen approached behind her and filled in the details as though he'd read her mind. "No caffeine, no artificial colors."

Feeling guilty that she'd just been talking about Owen to Hank, Victoria glanced over her shoulder to where Hank had been standing.

He was gone.

Before she could think too much about it, the door jangled again and Charles entered, carrying his twins, Aaron and Brianne, one in each arm. He addressed

Owen. "Dad's going to meet us for supper. He's on his way."

"Would you like a large table, then?" Victoria asked, quickly snapping back into work mode.

"Please. There will be six of us, if Owen and Paige are joining us."

Owen nodded and glanced around, as though he wanted to confirm that Paige was planning to eat with them.

Their daughter had slipped away. "She must have gone to hang up her jacket." Victoria grabbed a stack of menus and led them toward the dining room. "I'm sure she'll be right back down." She grabbed a couple of booster seats for the twins, and Charles looked grateful not to have to juggle both of them any longer. "I'll bring your father over when he arrives."

For the next several minutes, the bells on the door kept up a near-continual racket as customers filed in. If it hadn't been for the strange conversation with Hank weighing on her, Victoria would have grinned from ear to ear. They had a full house already, and it was still early.

Britney and Charlotte got busy taking orders and Victoria turned her attention to the kitchen, keeping one eye on the front door. Just as she began to wonder when Paige might reappear, the door jangled again, and Burke Hennessy stepped in with his wife, Christina, and their baby daughter Georgina.

Swallowing back fear, Victoria stepped out and

greeted them, frantically trying to think how she might get them to an empty table without walking past Charles. Given the scene Burke had made at the Saint Patrick's celebration when he'd called for Charles's arrest, Victoria feared what might happen if the two of them spotted each other inside her restaurant.

"Oh, look at Georgina!" Victoria cooed at the baby in an adorable dress. "She's getting so big." While she kept Christina distracted talking about her baby, Victoria glanced at the table where Charles sat in plain sight, and wondered if there would be a way to discreetly move him to a corner table without the Hennessys realizing what she was up to.

"She's over a year old now," Christina announced, beaming.

As she spoke, the bells on the door gave another rattle, and Aiden Fitzgerald walked in.

"One moment." Hoping to quickly sweep Aiden off toward Charles and move the doctor to another table in one fell swoop, Victoria stepped around Christina. She took Aiden by the arm. "Right this way."

They were halfway through the first dining room when a voice thundered behind her.

"Do all the Fitzgeralds in Fitzgerald Bay get seated first?" Burke Hennessy had followed them into the crowded room. "They really do own the whole town, don't they?"

Victoria wished she could hide behind the menus

she clutched. She spun around and faced Burke. "I'm sorry, he—"

But the lawyer wouldn't let her get any further. He boomed on in his courtroom voice. "The Fitzgeralds *do* own this town, don't they? They get the best service. Preferential treatment." He strode between the tables as if before a jury, and came to a stop just above Aaron's and Brianne's innocent heads. He glowered at Charles across the two-year-old twins. "It seems Fitzgeralds can get away with *murder.*"

There was nowhere to hide. The patrons from the back dining room got up from their seats and watched from the next doorway. Others turned their chairs so they could see. Even Charlotte and Britney had given up taking orders and watched with pale faces as Aiden Fitzgerald stomped toward Burke.

"That's quite enough!" the police chief demanded. "The investigation—"

He didn't get any further before Burke continued, jabbing a finger at Victoria. "You're on their payroll too, aren't you, honey? Or you'd like to be. Let me assure you, Miss Evans, seating Aiden Fitzgerald before me won't ever make you good enough for their family. You weren't good enough for them ten years ago. Why would you think they've changed?"

Mortified, Victoria looked around her, fearful that Paige had heard. The rest of the town she could live with, but she didn't want Paige to hear. But her little girl was nowhere in sight. Hadn't she been gone for a while? What had happened to her?

Aiden flagged his arms in the air as though he could erase everything Burke had just said. "Don't drag her into this! Your argument is with me, not her."

"My argument is on behalf of her and every other innocent in Fitzgerald Bay whose rights have been trampled by the Fitzgeralds!"

While Burke yelled back at Aiden, Victoria slipped between tables on her way to the door. Where was Paige? She'd been gone at least fifteen minutes. Her heart rate kicked higher. Her daughter had been so excited to share the details of her trip to the movies. It wasn't like her to disappear—especially not when she had interesting news to share.

Turning her back on the angry mayoral candidates, Victoria made it as far as the kitchen before she felt a hand on her arm.

She spun around. "Owen!" She immediately thought about Hank's insistence that Owen was guilty—that Owen was out to chase her from town.

"Where are you going?"

"I need to find Paige."

"She's been gone for more than ten minutes." Owen nodded as though he'd been thinking exactly the same thing. "I just checked the back dining room. She's not here."

"She's not in the kitchen, either."

Victoria opened the back door and looked around. No sign of Paige.

"Look." Owen pointed downward to a bowl of milk. "She's been feeding the cat again. It looks fresh. We must have just missed her."

"She's not here anymore. Maybe she went to her room." Victoria bounded up the back stairs, hoping that Paige was simply late because she'd taken the time to feed the cat. Surely she'd find her upstairs.

Victoria swept into their apartment and checked everywhere. No sign of Paige or her jacket. She spun back around and found Owen had followed her up.

"No sign of her."

"I don't think she ever came up here," Owen observed. "Her fingers were sticky with chocolate, but the doorknob is clean."

Much as Victoria would have loved to attribute the clean doorknob to her daughter's conscientious hand-washing, she knew Paige too well. "Where could she have gone? Most of Main Street is closed by now."

Owen clasped Victoria by the shoulders. His touch was gentle, yet firm. So different from the hold Hank had placed on her shoulder earlier.

"She had her phone with her. Can you try calling her?"

Victoria had been so worried that she hadn't thought of that. She fished around in her spacious apron pockets for her phone. "One text message," she read aloud, and then gasped when she saw what it was.

"What?" Owen pulled closer.

"It's from Paige." She showed him the screen with trembling hands.

HUMMING MAN IN TRUCK HELP

FOURTEEN

Owen stared at the message and tried frantically to think. His daughter was in a truck with the humming perpetrator he'd tried to chase down?

Victoria raced down the back stairs and landed in the kitchen just in time to see Burke and Christina stalk out the front door, taking part of the evening crowd with them.

Aiden approached her. "I'm sorry—" he began.

"Put out an alert," Owen interrupted his father and darted out the front door, past the leaving customers, in the direction of the police station. "Paige has been kidnapped."

"What?" Aiden staggered back.

"Paige sent this—" Victoria showed Aiden the text message. "When my safe was broken into three weeks ago, Paige overheard the burglar humming 'The Wreck of the Edmund Fitzgerald.' She's been trying to help us find the man ever since. I tried to tell her safety is more important than catching him, but—"

Victoria broke off as Owen bounded back in with a police radio in his hand.

"All units, calling all units." He broadcast news of the disappearance, including a description of Paige and what she'd been wearing when she'd disappeared.

"I've got all that," Keira's impatient voice radioed back. "*Who* are we looking for?"

"Paige Fitzgerald." Owen grimaced. "Evans. My daughter."

Victoria's eyes widened at Owen's inadvertent disclosure and she looked at Aiden.

The police chief didn't blink. "We'll find her."

Charlotte appeared by Victoria's side. "Go. Look. Britney and I can cover the restaurant."

Victoria wanted to protest, but several of the customers had left with the Hennessys and none of the others looked the least bit impatient about getting their food. In fact, a couple of high school guys leaped up from a nearby table.

"We'll help you look," the taller one announced, pulling out his keys and charging out the door.

"Me, too." Charles scooped up the twins. "They're not hungry after all that popcorn anyway. We'll drive around. I'll call if I see anything."

While officers checked in with Owen over the radio, announcing which areas they were covering, a few more determined-looking citizens brandished their car keys and headed out with promises to do their best to bring Paige back safe and sound.

Victoria looked at the phone in her hand. Maybe it was a long shot, but if Paige had been able to send off a text message, then, at least until recently, she still had use of her phone. Typing quickly, Victoria shot her daughter a text.

WHERE R U

She stared at the tiny screen and prayed while people swarmed around her. Owen continued to relay tactical messages, checking in with the units on patrol. Aiden declared he was headed back across the street to set up a command center at the police station, and Britney insisted on calling Clint and asking him to help with the search.

Then a message arrived from Paige.

BARN

"She's in a barn!" Victoria screamed. "Paige sent me a message—she's in a barn."

Owen gripped her shoulders. "Where?"

Hardly able to control her trembling fingers, Victoria sent another message.

WHERE

She bit her lips and waited, praying frantically. The response came quickly.

IDK

"I don't know," Victoria translated.

"Come on." Owen grabbed her arm and pulled her out the door. "Keep asking questions. Ask her about landmarks." They piled into his Raptor pickup and Owen headed out of town.

While Victoria snapped on her seat belt, before she could ask another question, a text came back.

HANK

"Hank." Victoria grabbed Owen's arm. "But he lives in town. He doesn't have a barn."

Having left the town behind, Owen turned onto a side road. "He doesn't, but his father does."

"Ronald Monroe." Victoria whispered the name of the retired judge who lived on the outskirts of town in his family's ancestral estate. Something else clicked about the location. "He lives just off Mayflower Road."

Owen took his eyes off the road just long enough to meet her eyes. He shifted the truck into a higher gear and it bounced forward.

"Hank was on duty tonight," Victoria realized aloud. "Did he check in?"

"No."

"But he would have heard everything you said over the police radio."

"So he knows we're looking for Paige."

The pickup topped a hill. The Monroe estate lay around the next bend in the road. "What are we going to do? We don't want to make Hank nervous—what if he does something to hurt Paige?"

Owen brought the truck to a stop on the edge of the road near thick tree cover a few feet from where the Monroe driveway began. "Will Hank talk to you?"

"Yes." Victoria quickly realized that she needed

Owen to know what Hank had said earlier. "Owen, Hank was at the Sugar Plum just before you came in with Paige. He told me those were *your* muddy fingerprints on the wall last weekend. He said he needed my help getting your fingerprints again to convict you."

Owen's eyes flashed with Irish temper. "I should have realized it sooner. That's why Hank never denied the rumors all this time."

"Why?"

"Because he was the one spreading them. Can you drive my truck?"

Though she wasn't entirely certain she understood all that Owen was saying, Victoria looked at the manual transmission. "No problem."

"I'll hop out here, call my brothers and get them in on the plan, and head in on foot. You drive up, tell Hank you came alone and get him talking, maybe even get him to explain what he's been up to. Try to get Paige away from him, but most of all buy us time until backup arrives. The rest of us will circle around and close in on him."

"Then what?" She met Owen's eyes.

"Once Paige is safe, we'll apprehend Hank."

Victoria gripped Owen's hand. "Do you think it's going to be that easy?"

"Let's pray."

They uttered a quick, heartfelt prayer for Paige's safety and a peaceful resolution to their troubles. As they whispered a hasty "amen," Owen met her eyes.

Before she could blink, he leaned forward and kissed her. "You'll do fine. We'll get her back."

Then Owen hopped out of the truck and Victoria put it in gear, driving up the long driveway, frantically trying to think of what she could possibly say to Hank Monroe.

Had he kidnapped Paige? Or had she stowed away in his truck by mistake? Was Hank really the humming man who'd broken into her safe? How many of the other incidents at the Sugar Plum might he have been behind?

And most important, how was she going to get Paige away from him?

Owen used his phone to call his brothers and Keira as he made his way through the dense trees toward the Monroe barn. Was his daughter in there? Was she scared? Injured? He needed to get to her. He hadn't even had a chance to tell her he was her father. Would he ever have an opportunity to tell her the truth?

Ducking back behind a large oak tree, Owen peeked out. He watched as Victoria drove his truck toward the barn.

"Hello?" she called out as she parked the truck and slid out.

"Hello." A single bulb flickered on above the barn doors, and Hank stepped into the halo of light with Paige under his arm.

Owen's heart clenched. His daughter! He had to

protect her! But he couldn't risk upsetting Hank. Much as he wanted to tackle him flat, there was nothing he could do but stay out of sight and ask God to watch over them all.

"I had a stowaway in my truck," Hank growled at Victoria.

"I'm sorry about that. I'll take her home now." Victoria took a step closer.

"Not so fast! I didn't realize until she showed up in my truck how very useful she could be." Hank licked his lips. "You and I are supposed to be together, Victoria. I've always known we're supposed to be together. But you didn't agree with me, did you?"

"Hank, we can talk about this. Please, let Paige go."

"No!" Hank shouted, and for the first time, Owen realized the man held a gun.

"Owen's here, isn't he?"

"I—I came alone."

"That's his truck." Hank looked about warily, then called loudly, "Owen?"

Deliberating whether he should respond, Owen kept his mouth shut.

"It doesn't matter." Hank pulled something out of his pocket. "I should have given you this earlier. It's a copy of an email Owen sent to Cooper Hennessy."

"How did you get a copy of Owen's email?" Victoria's voice carried clearly.

"We share an office."

Though Owen had always been cautious about logging off whenever he was away from his computer, he chided himself for not considering the possibility that Hank might have learned his password by watching him type it in. Armed with Owen's password, Hank could have accessed his personal account from anywhere—he wouldn't even have needed his computer.

Worse yet, Owen was nearly certain he knew which email Hank had printed off to share with Victoria— his angry and determined plan to take Victoria to court for joint custody.

He watched Victoria's face as she read the fluttering paper. She looked pale, as did Paige, standing frozen, eyes wide, with Hank's hand clamping her shoulder.

"You see, he was never going to let you keep her. Never." Hank grinned. "But I can help you. All you need to do is gather evidence against Owen. He can go to jail, and you and I can be together, just like everyone thinks we have been all these years."

With white-knuckled fingers, Owen gripped the stone outcropping of the old fence line he was hiding behind. He had to do something. Paige looked as if she was going to pass out. Surely backup had arrived by now, or would soon. They knew not to buzz his radio for fear Hank might overhear. Though he saw no sign of them anywhere, he had to trust they were keeping out of sight so Hank wouldn't see them, either.

"We can talk about this, Hank." Victoria's voice stayed steady, most likely in an effort to keep Paige calm. "But I think Paige would be more comfortable with me."

"So you think I'm just going to hand her over? She climbed in my truck herself—thought she was going to catch the bad guy. I'm not the bad guy!" he shouted. "Owen's the bad guy! He stole you from me! Those stupid Fitzgeralds think they run this town. They think they can have whatever they want, but they can't. Owen can't have you, and he can't have Paige."

Hank raised his sidearm as he finished speaking, and Owen watched as if in slow motion as the man's finger moved against the trigger.

He was about to shoot Victoria!

"No!" Owen leaped over the wall, out into the open, not caring whether backup had arrived, not caring about anything but stopping Hank from shooting the woman he loved.

Hank's hand moved as he depressed the trigger, and the shots flew in Owen's direction, kicking up dirt on the hillside.

Owen dived down the slope, hoping to tear the gun from Hank's hand, or distract the man enough for Paige to get free.

"Owen." Hank trained the gun on him, and Owen realized that if the man took a shot now, he wouldn't miss. "So nice of you to join us. You're just in time to die."

"You can't kill him!" Victoria screamed and stepped forward.

Hank kept the gun trained on Owen, but glanced back at her.

"You can't kill him *here*." She stepped forward, thinking quickly. Could she make Hank think she was on his side? "You'd get caught—and the evidence would point to you."

A sly grin formed on Hank's face. "You're right. I knew you were a smart girl. We've got to make it look like someone else did it." He let go of Paige's shoulders and snapped his fingers. "Charles. We'll frame him. Burke Hennessy has been calling for his head. All he needs is a charge that will stick. I can fake the evidence just like I planned to fake Owen's fingerprints at the Sugar Plum crime scene. The Fitzgeralds will go down in shame and the Monroe family will rule this town. My father has been talking about running for mayor. We can change the name to Monroe Bay."

"That's a great idea." Victoria kept her eyes on her daughter. Paige was scared, no doubt about it, but she met her mother's eyes, and Victoria winked at her. "I have the keys to Owen's truck. Do you want them?"

"Yeah. Bring them here."

Victoria hesitated. Hank was highly unstable, and he'd already shown her how trigger-happy he was. She had to use whatever advantage she had. "Just give me Paige and you can have the keys."

Hank's eyes narrowed. "Give me the keys! I have a gun!"

"If you want the keys—" Owen jumped into the conversation "—let Paige go."

"Are you stupid?" Hank shot the ground in front of Owen—a warning shot.

Victoria nearly threw the keys at him at that instant, but realized that would give him every advantage. Where was the backup Owen had been going to call in? Were they waiting for Paige to step away so they could get a clear shot at Hank? She had to get her daughter away from the man.

"I'll give you the keys," Victoria offered, "and Owen will get into the truck."

"No! He has to be tied up first." Hank appeared to be losing his temper even more than he already had.

"I can tie him up," Victoria offered. "Do you have rope?"

"In the barn."

"Okay." Victoria scooted past Hank. It was dark, and she didn't see any sort of rope inside the barn. She spotted a lone bulb with a pull chain dangling from the hayloft near the rear of the barn. Darting forward, she gave it a yank, and light filled the barn.

The back of the barn was dusty, as though no one ever went there, but a row of footprints led to a large old tarp that looked as though it covered a car. Sure enough, tires peeked out from underneath. Whitewall. Who drove whitewalls anymore? She chided herself, realizing from the level of grime on the tarp that likely no one had driven the vehicle under it for a decade or more.

But Hank Monroe had driven a car with whitewall

tires back in high school—his white Mustang that his father had bought him for his sixteenth birthday.

A white car.

Under a tarp.

On Mayflower Road.

Heart thudding, Victoria silently lifted the tarp and looked underneath.

The white paint was dented and scratched and streaked with red.

"Hurry up with that rope!" Hank shouted from outside.

Victoria dropped the tarp, grabbed a length of rope hanging from a hook above her and headed for the door. She didn't dare waste any more time. Something told her the man who'd killed her father ten years ago wouldn't hesitate to kill again.

"I found the rope!" she announced quickly, before Hank lost his patience entirely.

"Good. Tie him up real tight. Bring him over here so I can make sure you do it right."

Victoria focused on keeping her hands steady as she wrapped the rope around Owen's wrists to Hank's barking specifications. Much as she'd have liked to do something sneaky that would allow Owen to get away later, she didn't know any sneaky rope tricks. And Hank was watching her too closely to allow her to get away with them even if she had.

"All right. Good enough," Hank growled. "Now hand me the keys."

"You're going to give me my daughter."

"I was thinking about that…" Hank began.

Victoria's heart plummeted.

"If I leave you two here, you might try something funny. So you're coming, too."

"J-just me, right?" Victoria's voice shook. "Paige can stay."

"No! Paige can't stay. Get in the truck!" Hank shoved Paige forward.

Victoria wrapped her arms around her daughter as they stumbled toward the waiting vehicle. She didn't want to go. If they left with Hank, anything might happen. She met Owen's eyes for just a second.

He tipped his head slightly forward as though urging them on, as though he was trying to communicate that they needed to hurry.

What was it he'd told her earlier? To get Paige out of the way so their backup could take Hank down?

Victoria guided her daughter around the front of the pickup. "Let's get in on the passenger side, Paige." She kept her daughter tucked under her arm, as though she could shield her with her body from whatever was about to happen.

And she was certain something was about to happen.

FIFTEEN

Owen waited until Paige and Victoria were safely around the vehicle, shielded by its thick metal sides, before he flew into action.

As Hank gave him a shove in the direction of the truck, Owen twisted his torso around, throwing himself backward against Hank in an attempt to force him to the ground.

For a moment, Hank fumbled, dropped a knee and appeared to be halfway down.

But without the use of his arms to hold him, Owen had no way of keeping him down. If only Victoria hadn't tied his hands so tight! He blew back a round kick with his left leg, but Hank caught him by the ankle before he even made contact, and jerked up on his foot.

Owen went down, face-planting in the dirt.

Hank was on him immediately.

Did the lawman know he was likely surrounded by his fellow police officers, who were only awaiting a clean shot to take him down? Hank acted as though he suspected he might be—he never let himself become separated from Owen's side, even as he pulled him roughly to his feet and shoved him instead into the barn.

"I thought we were leaving," Owen reminded him.

"Change of plans. If you won't go nicely, we're going to have to stay right here."

Hank kept an arm around him as he pulled him deeper into the darkness of the barn.

Victoria was relieved to see Owen's sister Keira, the rookie of the FBPD, crouching behind Owen's truck, waiting for them. Keira gestured for them to stay low while she talked to the other officers via cell phone.

"Somebody's got to go in." Keira paused. "Well, who is Hank most likely to listen to? He already said he thinks the Fitzgeralds are corrupt." Another pause. "We don't have time to get a negotiator in there. Hank hates Owen—he already said so. We have to do something *now*. Owen's life depends on it."

Victoria quickly realized what Keira and her fellow officers, who must have been hidden around the perimeter of the property, were discussing. Hank had taken Owen hostage, but without any real reason to keep him alive, Hank might lose his temper completely and shoot Owen at any moment.

"I'll go in." Victoria gave Paige another squeeze. "Get Paige to safety."

"But you don't—" Keira began to protest.

"Hank's on the brink. I could see it in his eyes. Someone's got to talk to him, and I'm the only one he'll listen to."

"Mommy!" Paige reached for her, fear in her eyes.

"I love you, Paige. Don't worry. Keira will keep you safe."

"She's my aunt, isn't she? And Owen is my dad? I heard him over the radio."

"Yes, sweetheart, Owen is your dad. He and I love you very much. Right now I need to talk to Hank about your dad, okay?"

Warm trust filled her daughter's eyes, and she stepped back toward Keira. "Okay."

Victoria ran around the front of the truck before she could change her mind. "Hank?" she called out as she approached the barn door. She figured Hank didn't *know* he was surrounded, though he likely suspected it. If she could convince him they were the only ones around, that she was willing to go along with his plans…well, it was a long shot, but it was all she had.

"Hank? I thought we were leaving?"

"There's been a change of plans."

Victoria stood in the doorway and let her eyes adjust to the relative dim of the barn. She couldn't see either of the men, but she could hear heavy breathing. What was Hank doing with Owen? "I thought you wanted to frame Charles?"

She heard Hank spit. "Owen won't cooperate."

Thoughts racing, Victoria tried to think of what

she could say to lure the men out of the barn. Owen's brothers couldn't go after Hank until they knew Owen was out of the line of fire. She had to get them out in the open. "Come on, Hank, let's just throw him in the back of the truck and get going. He's tied up. You're bigger than he is."

Silence. She could almost hear Hank wrestling with what to do next. "What do you care, anyway?" he growled finally. "I thought you just wanted your girl back?"

Forcing all her anger into her voice, Victoria tried to think of something that would convince Hank to trust her enough to leave the barn. "If I leave with Paige, Owen's just going to turn around and try to get custody of her. I can't let that happen. I need your help to get Owen out of the picture for good."

A motion in the back of the barn caught her attention, and Hank pulled on the light above the tarp-covered Mustang, revealing both men standing in front of the car. Hank held a gun to Owen's head.

The sight sent Victoria's heart rate skyrocketing.

Hank's wicked smile was deeply shadowed by the overhead light. "Should I kill him?"

"Not here. If you leave behind any evidence, his death could be traced to you. Let's take him to Charles's place. But hurry. Charles was at the Sugar Plum. If we wait too long, he might get home and catch you in the act."

"Okay," Hank agreed finally. "But first, Owen, there's something I want you to see."

Owen braced himself. Hank was in a desperate corner and was likely to act irrationally. Victoria obviously didn't understand the danger she was dealing with. Why had she returned? She should have escaped with Paige. Now they were both in danger.

The moment Hank had pulled him back through the doorway, Owen had realized the man had no intention of letting him leave the barn alive. With heart-crushing gratitude, he realized that Victoria had come back for him. She knew she was the only person who had any shot at talking to Hank.

Too bad Hank was in no mood to listen to anybody.

Hank took a step back and pulled away the tarp behind them. For the first time, Owen was able to see what it had been covering.

"Your Mustang. Were you in an accident, Hank?"

"You might say that. It wasn't so much an accident as on purpose, though."

Owen didn't figure there was anything to be gained by playing dumb. Hank wouldn't have shown him the car if he hadn't wanted to rub his nose in what he'd done to his cousin. "Why'd you do it? Why kill Patrick? He never did anything against you."

"It wasn't supposed to be Patrick." Hank snarled. "That old drunk Stanley Evans wanted me to stop talking about Victoria. He thought he could blackmail me into shutting my mouth. I had to show him."

"Blackmail?" Owen asked. "What kind of blackmail?"

"You think I'm stupid?" Hank grabbed him by the arm and shoved him toward the door. "You think I'm going to tell you? No way. You're going to die." He waved the gun at Victoria. "Let's get going!"

Victoria ran toward Owen's truck, her heart crushed. Her dad had tried to quiet Hank's rumors? He'd died trying to protect her? And all these years she'd been ashamed of him. Tears leaked down her cheeks, but as she cleared the passenger side of the vehicle, she saw with relief that Paige was gone, hopefully taken somewhere safe by Keira.

She pushed back the tears and turned to face Hank as he pushed Owen ahead of him toward the truck. Though she couldn't see Owen's brothers anywhere, she knew they had to be close by, waiting for an opening to act. But they couldn't do anything until Hank moved his gun from Owen's back. If Hank got a single shot off, Owen would die.

"Do you want the keys?" she asked from the passenger side of the vehicle, as Hank pushed Owen toward the driver's door.

"Toss 'em here." Hank tucked his gun into the back of his waistband, took two steps away from Owen and held out his hands.

Victoria held his eye contact as she slowly dipped her arms forward, preparing to toss the keys. If the waiting officers were ever going to get an opening, this was it. She'd keep Hank distracted for as many seconds as she could, but she couldn't let him become suspicious, nor could she give him a chance to realize that Paige wasn't with them anymore.

"Ready?"

He nodded, looking mildly impatient, but didn't look away from the keys.

She let them fly gently through the air.

Just as Hank's hands closed around them, Douglas and Ryan Fitzgerald leaped from the darkness and grabbed him from each side.

Victoria ducked instinctively behind the truck, unwilling to watch what might happen next.

A moment later, Owen was beside her, slipping off the rope one of the swarming officers had evidently cut. Victoria could hear Ryan attempting to Mirandize Hank, who insisted with strong language that he was already more than aware of his rights.

Owen wrapped his arms around her and pulled her against his shoulder. Only then did she realize how badly she was shaking.

"Are you okay?"

She buried her face against his shoulder, gripping his strong arms tightly, hardly able to believe he'd made it through unscathed. "I'm okay. Are you okay?"

"Thanks to you. Where's Paige?"

"I left her with Keira."

"Let's go find her."

They took a few trembling steps toward the woods.

"Mommy!"

Paige flew forward, and Victoria caught her daughter up in her arms. As she held her tight, Paige looked over her shoulder at Owen.

Owen smiled sheepishly at his daughter.

"I heard you on the radio," Paige began quietly, almost as though she was afraid he might deny the truth of what he'd said before.

"I'm your father, Paige."

"Yes!" Paige dropped her hold on Victoria and leaped for Owen, who caught her up in a tight bear hug.

Victoria took a step back, but Owen pulled her toward them again.

The police captain, Douglas Fitzgerald, approached, and Owen addressed him from over the top of his daughter's head. "The white Mustang under the tarp is critical evidence I want to go over with you. And we'll need to follow up with Hank. There's more to this story than he's told us."

"Of course." Douglas turned to address Victoria. "Thank you for your assistance. I wouldn't have let you go in if I'd had a chance to stop you, but—" he looked at his brother and swallowed "—I'm glad you did what you did. You gave us the break we needed to apprehend Hank, and you saved my little brother's life."

* * *

Back at the Sugar Plum, the searchers who'd returned sent up a cheer when Victoria carried her daughter through the front door.

Clint waved from the kitchen. "I've got everything under control. Take your time."

Victoria mouthed a thank-you to him and stopped to thank everyone who had gone out to help search for her daughter.

By the time she'd served everyone and put her exhausted daughter to bed, Victoria was ready to crumple into a ball herself. Just as she was about to lock up for the night, the bell on the door jangled and Owen walked in, looking every bit as tired as she felt.

He set a familiar red bank bag on top of the pastry case.

Victoria's jaw dropped. "Is it mine? The one that was stolen?"

"We found it under the tarp with the car. We counted the money—it's exactly one hundred dollars less than the amount you reported stolen."

"I can only assume he used the missing hundred as the one-hundred dollar bill he offered me the next day." Pulling the zipper back gingerly, Victoria peeked inside to see the report she'd run just a few weeks before, along with the cash and checks. "Praise the Lord. This should cover my expenses."

"God provided." Owen gave her a tired smile. "And Paige was right. Hank was humming 'The Wreck of the Edmund Fitzgerald.' He was upset with me for stealing you away from him. His plan was to scare you enough that you'd turn to him for help, and he could blame all your troubles on me. Hank was the shadowy figure you've seen lurking outside your windows. You're safe now."

The story fit with everything Hank had said to her, right down to the end. She walked with Owen back into the kitchen and stashed the bank bag securely inside the new safe. "Did you ever learn what was behind the blackmail story with my dad?"

Owen let out a long breath. "Hank was running moonshine for Frank Gallagher, and your father knew it. Your father got sick of the rumors Hank was spreading about you. He told Hank if he didn't come clean and clear up your reputation, he'd let everybody know he'd been running shine, which would have not only ruined Hank's reputation as a good kid, but since he was eighteen, it would have stayed on his record, and probably kept him from ever fulfilling his plans of getting hired as a cop. Hank flew into a rage, chased your dad off his property and rammed him into Patrick's car. Then Hank hid the Mustang in the barn and lit out of town. When he learned you'd left town the same night, he called all his friends and told them the two of you had run away together."

Victoria hung her head. "All these years—" she sniffled away a tear "—I was so ashamed of my father. But in reality, he died defending me." Her tired mind sputtered and she shook her head. "What about Judge Monroe? That Mustang has been parked on his property for a decade. Is he going to go to jail for concealing evidence?"

"He claims he never went out to the barn, and had no idea there was anything under a tarp out there."

"For ten years? How could he possibly be that oblivious?"

"We have no way of proving otherwise." Owen reached for her. "I talked to my family members and explained everything. I hope you don't mind—after I gave away the truth over the radio, there didn't seem to be any point in waiting to explain things together."

Victoria tried to relax as his hand settled on her shoulder, but she still felt wary of trusting Owen. "What about the email Hank showed me? He said you wrote those words." She watched his face intently, begging him to deny that it was true.

Owen's guilty expression did nothing to bolster her confidence. "I was hurt and angry back then. I—"

She felt fear rising in her throat. Everything was far from over. "Are you going to take me to court?"

Owen let go of her shoulder and took a step back. "I still need to talk to Cooper—"

"I agreed to let you have shared custody of Paige," she reminded him. "You don't have to put Paige through this. It won't change anything."

"I'm not going to fight you." Owen met her eyes, but

his words were less than encouraging. "Tomorrow's Sunday. Can I come by and get Paige after church?"

"She'd really like that. She's been talking about you nonstop." Victoria watched as he walked toward the door. She could tell that he was exhausted, and she was dead on her feet as well, but she wished he'd answer more of her questions before leaving.

"It's going to be okay." Owen turned back as he gripped the door handle. "I promise."

After church, Owen raced over to the Sugar Plum, reaching it before it opened for the Sunday lunch crowd. He caught Victoria on her way out of the fridge and grabbed the magnet off the wall. "I thought so."

"What?" Victoria looked startled by his sudden appearance.

"It says, 'The truth shall set you free.'" Owen grinned. Finally, everything began to make sense. "Were you listening to the sermon today?"

"Of course. Pastor Larch talked about Jesus being the Way, the Truth and the Life."

"Jesus is the Truth," Owen repeated. "Ever since you told me about Paige, I've been so upset that you kept her from me all these years, but it isn't just telling the truth that sets us free, it's Christ Himself."

"I don't understand."

Owen placed the magnet reverently on the refrigerator and cupped her shoulders in his hands. "I've been hiding from God, running from faith ever since

Patrick died. I wasn't in any position to be a father, not without a relationship with my heavenly Father to guide me."

"What are you saying?" Victoria looked up at him with trust simmering in her warm brown eyes.

"I'm saying, even if I'd known about Paige from day one, what kind of father would I have been? I didn't even have faith." He leaned close until his forehead touched hers. "I'm saying, it's okay. I'm not happy that you hid Paige from me, but it turned out okay. I'm saying, I forgive you."

Victoria smiled up at him. The tears that shimmered in her eyes didn't leak down her cheeks this time. "There it is."

"There what is?" he asked.

"The exhilarating feeling of freedom I expected to feel once I told you the truth."

He took a deep breath. He could almost feel it, too. "Do you forgive me, too?"

"What for?"

"For writing that stupid email to Cooper, for losing my temper..."

"You do have a bit of an Irish temper." She planted a kiss near his lips. "Of course I forgive you. I—" Her confession broke off as Paige bounded into the room.

"Whoa. Should I come back later?" Paige backed toward the stairs as the two of them leaped apart.

"No, come on in." Owen extended an arm toward

her. "I was wondering if you'd like to do some shopping with me this afternoon."

"Are we going to the Reading Nook?"

"Something even better."

Owen took Paige to the jewelry store for her expert input before stopping by the Hennessy Law Office for his appointment with Cooper. He'd already given Cooper his income information the week before, so when he'd called after church to ask him to calculate what his back child support payments should have been for the past decade, Cooper had assured him that he'd have the figures ready in time to meet with him that afternoon.

Paige waited patiently, admiring the necklace he'd bought her, while Owen went over the numbers with Cooper. It would mean liquidating some assets and draining his savings, but Owen felt confident he'd be able to pay Victoria what he owed her. Then she'd have a solid financial cushion so she wouldn't have to worry anymore about keeping her business afloat. And with everything square between them, he prayed she'd have a different answer to the question he was burning to ask again.

Victoria carried a package of sausage from the walk-in freezer for the Ballycastle sausage rolls that would be on special that evening. Hefting the heavy vacuum-sealed bag onto her shoulder, she gave the freezer handle a tug, walked through the fridge and pulled open the door.

Odd.

It smelled like gasoline in her kitchen.

And the floor looked wet.

She'd been in the freezer only a few minutes, shuffling around boxes of frozen meats and vegetables to find the sausage she needed. What could have happened in that short amount of time? No one was around at this time in the afternoon, except Charlotte, who was supposed to be upstairs making up the rooms after their weekend guests had departed. Even Paige had gone off with Owen.

As she stood in the doorway of the fridge, something rattled across the floor from the direction of the back door. Victoria blinked at the object, which looked like a glass beer bottle but appeared to be smoking from the top.

Had someone thrown a bomb inside her restaurant?

For a second, she considered kicking it back out the door, but instead she dived back into the fridge, letting the door slam shut behind her as the crude explosive detonated, rattling the kitchen with its searing blast.

As he shook hands with Cooper en route to the front door, Owen heard the sound of sirens. Who was in trouble now?

He ran to the doorway in time to see a fire truck tearing up Main Street. The fire engine groaned to a halt in front of the Sugar Plum Café. As uniformed firemen leaped out and ran toward the building, Owen spotted the thick black smoke that belched up from the building's back side.

The smoke was coming from the kitchen.

"Victoria!" Owen's heart tore and he scooped Paige into his arms, running with her down the street to find a second fire engine already parked around the corner, the firemen out, their hoses running.

How long had they been at work? Owen had been deep in conversation, oblivious to anything beyond Paige in the waiting room.

He tore around the corner and saw his cousins Danny and Liam Fitzgerald among the firefighters on the scene. "Where's Victoria?" he shouted.

Liam shook his head.

"Owen, get back." Fiona appeared from somewhere behind him, pulling on his arm, dragging him away from the black smoke that poured from a shattered window.

"Take Paige." He handed his daughter to his sister.

"Daddy?"

"It's going to be okay. I'm going to get your mom."

Paige looked at him with wide, trusting eyes, as though she had no doubt he'd come through on his promise.

He had to.

He turned to Danny and Liam. "Where's Victoria?" This time he got in their faces.

"The smoke's too thick to see," Danny explained, turning to focus on the hose he was working with.

Owen realized he couldn't distract the men while they were working. He spotted Charlotte on the edge of the crowd.

"Did Victoria get out?"

Tears streamed down the older woman's face. "They can't find her. I think she was in the kitchen. That's where the fire started. It blew up so fast—one of the firemen already said he suspects it was arson." She shook her head apologetically. "The fire filled the kitchen doorway all the way to the back door. She never had a chance."

No! Owen wanted to scream to the sky. A couple of firefighters in full gear stomped back outside from the back kitchen door.

"Where's Victoria?" He got in their faces, unmindful of the thick smoke that billowed everywhere. "Did you find her?"

The masked men simply shook their heads.

"Daddy?" Paige called from Fiona's arms.

Owen looked back at his daughter. He couldn't let her grow up without a mother. He knew how much it had hurt Victoria to lose her mother. He wouldn't let his little girl go through that, not if there was anything he could do about it.

Darting past the exiting firemen, Owen gulped a breath and plunged through the smoke into the kitchen. He'd spent enough time in the place to have the layout memorized, so as he pinched his eyes shut against the stinging smoke, he felt along the scorched back wall for the handle to the walk-in fridge and pulled it open.

He could just make out the items on the shelves through the smoke.

Pulling the door shut behind him to keep the smoke from overtaking him, he plunged through to the freezer door.

Victoria shivered in the corner, but she threw herself at him and held him tight, coughing. "Is it safe to come out?"

He smoothed down her hair and held her tight. "Safe enough."

Not wanting to make Paige wait another second to see her mother, Owen scooped Victoria up and shoved his way back out, through the black smoke, into the clear air of the sunny day.

He ran to Paige, who flew free of Fiona's arms and leaped at them. "Mommy! Mommy! I was so worried about you!"

"We were worried, too." Aiden Fitzgerald approached from just beyond Fiona's shoulder. "Miss Evans, I know some have suggested that our family looks down on you. And I'll admit, I am very protective of my children and the company they keep. But you have proven yourself to be a good Christian woman and a pillar of this community. We're tickled that little Paige—and both of you, really—are part of our family. Will you please overlook the sins of our past and forgive us for the way we treated you?"

"Of course."

"That's it." Owen dropped down on one knee.

"Are you okay?" Victoria gasped.

"I can't wait another minute." He pulled out the small velvet box that held the ring Paige had helped him pick out. "I need you in my life, Victoria. I love you. I've always loved you."

Victoria pulled him back up to standing. "Owen." She sniffled and pulled him close for a kiss.

He'd waited so long to kiss her—to really kiss her—that it took Owen several more moments before he realized she had yet to answer his question. He broke away from the kiss reluctantly. "Will you marry me?" he whispered, pressing his forehead against hers.

"Yes."

"Yes!" Paige squealed beside him. "We're going to be a family!"

Cheers erupted around them, and Owen turned to see his entire family had gathered on the street.

"Well done, Owen." Douglas clapped him on the back.

Keira gave a whoop and jumped in the air, and Ryan nodded his approval.

"I'm going to be a Fitzgerald!" Paige announced to them all.

"Welcome to the family," Fiona said with a smile, though her eyes looked troubled as she eyed the fire and murmured, "I hope our family can figure out who did this."

"You're sure you want to be a part of this family?" Owen asked Victoria in a whisper, knowing well that the Fitzgeralds—and all the troubles that had plagued them of late—could be a bit overwhelming at times.

"There's no family in the world I'd rather be a part of." And she kissed him again as if she meant it.

* * * * *

Dear Reader,

As you may have guessed from the fiery ending of Owen and Victoria's story, the adventures of the Fitzgerald family members are far from over. *The Detective's Secret Daughter* is the third of six books, each of which follows another member of the Fitzgerald family as they seek to uncover the truth behind Olivia Henry's murder, and the secrets in Fitzgerald Bay. I've posted a full list of the books in the series on my website, www.rachellemccalla.com.

While you're there, you might want to check out my recipe section, which is filled with treats from the Sugar Plum Café! From Irish meat-and-potato pie, to cutout sugar cookies, to fruit tarts, if you found the daily food specials at the Sugar Plum Café as tempting as Victoria's customers did, you might want to try making some of them yourself. Whether your taste buds tingled at the thought of the Cape Cod egg scramble, or you found yourself scrambling for an Irish soda bread recipe, you'll find all those recipes and more on my website. Just click on the link for recipes.

Besides the recipes for food, I hope you found Victoria and Owen's story to be a perfect recipe for love and family. May God bless you richly, and may all your recipes, whether for food or family, turn out just right.

Blessings,
Rachelle

Questions for Discussion

1. It took Victoria almost ten years to tell Owen about his daughter, Paige. How do you feel about her decision to tell Owen the truth when she did? Does the situation justify her choice? What would you have done in her shoes?

2. When Owen learns he has a daughter, he is determined to gain joint custody of her. How do you feel about his reaction? Does it make you respect him more, or less?

3. Victoria had long trusted that God used everything in her life—even the difficult times—as ingredients for the recipe He had planned for her life. But as her problems continue to multiply, she finds her faith is challenged. Have you experienced similar periods of trial and doubt in your own faith journey? What helped you through them? What aspects of Victoria's journey remind you of your own?

4. Owen feels frustrated by the many open cases and the time it's taking to solve them. Have you ever felt frustrated when something didn't come together as quickly as you'd hoped? How does

Owen cope with his frustration? Is there anything you can learn from his experiences?

5. Victoria moved Paige to Fitzgerald Bay in part to raise her daughter in a safe, peaceful place. But shortly after they arrive in town, that peacefulness is shattered by Olivia's murder. Have you ever sought peace only to have it evade you? Are we ever able to find perfect peace on this side of heaven? How does your faith in God sustain you when you can't find peace anywhere else?

6. Owen Fitzgerald and Hank Monroe have a lot in common: they both come from upstanding local families, they're both police officers and both have a thing for Victoria. Even Victoria has trouble sorting out which man can be trusted. Can we ever really know a person's true motives? What clues does Victoria use to help guide her? Have you ever felt betrayed by someone you thought you could trust? How did you recover from that betrayal?

7. Victoria is turned off by Hank's offers to help her. Why do you think she responds the way she does? Have you ever had a similar experience? How did her faith in God influence her choices? How does your faith influence your choices?

8. As Owen is contemplating his cousin Patrick's death and Victoria's insistence that her father had promised her he wouldn't drink and drive, Owen concludes that someone was lying. Who was really lying? How did Hank Monroe's lies affect individuals far beyond those he targeted? How do our lies—no matter how pure our motives when we make them—come back to haunt us? Is it ever okay to lie?

9. Victoria is forced to consider the possibility that her trusted employees, Charlotte and Britney, may have been conspiring against her to run her out of business. Have you ever been betrayed by a trusted friend? How did you respond? Do you agree with the way Victoria handled the situation? What else might she have done?

10. The members of Owen's extended family are people of faith. In the wake of Patrick's death and Victoria's disappearance, Owen felt as though he'd stuck his head in the sand, avoiding loving relationships with God and others. How does having a faithful family make it easier for him to react this way? In what ways does his family's faith help bring him back into a relationship with God?

11. Victoria decides not to press charges against Owen related to the crimes at the Sugar Plum.

Given the circumstances, do you think she made a prudent choice? What would you have done?

12. In the end, we learn that Victoria's often-drunk father actually had no alcohol in his system at the time of his accident with Patrick. How do you think this fact will influence the attitudes of the Fitzgeralds toward her once the truth becomes widely known? *Should* it make a difference? Is it wise to judge a person by his or her extended family? Why or why not?

13. Victoria allows Clint to help out at the Sugar Plum even though he is a prime suspect in the crimes against her. Do you agree with her choice? What advantages or disadvantages might accompany her decision?

14. As Owen comes to terms with the secret Victoria kept from him, he begins to realize why she hid Paige from him for so many years. How do you feel about his change in attitude? How do the Sunday sermons and scripture play a role in Owen's eventual change of heart?

15. As you think about the key verse, "The truth shall set you free" (*John* 8:32), in what ways do you see these words affecting Owen and Victoria? As you may recall, Victoria didn't feel "set free" when

she first told Owen the truth. Have you ever been disappointed by what happened when you told the truth? Did things eventually turn out for the best? How?

LARGER-PRINT BOOKS!

**GET 2 FREE
LARGER-PRINT NOVELS
PLUS 2 FREE
MYSTERY GIFTS**

Love Inspired.

SUSPENSE

RIVETING INSPIRATIONAL ROMANCE

Larger-print novels are now available...

YES! Please send me 2 FREE LARGER-PRINT Love Inspired® Suspense novels and my 2 FREE mystery gifts (gifts are worth about $10). After receiving them, if I don't wish to receive any more books, I can return the shipping statement marked "cancel". If I don't cancel, I will receive 4 brand-new novels every month and be billed just $4.99 per book in the U.S. or $5.49 per book in Canada. That's a saving of at least 23% off the cover price. It's quite a bargain! Shipping and handling is just 50¢ per book in the U.S. and 75¢ per book in Canada.* I understand that accepting the 2 free books and gifts places me under no obligation to buy anything. I can always return a shipment and cancel at any time. Even if I never buy another book, the two free books and gifts are mine to keep forever.

110/310 IDN FEH3

Name _____ (PLEASE PRINT) _____

Address _____ Apt. # _____

City _____ State/Prov. _____ Zip/Postal Code _____

Signature (if under 18, a parent or guardian must sign)

Mail to the **Reader Service**:
IN U.S.A.: P.O. Box 1867, Buffalo, NY 14240-1867
IN CANADA: P.O. Box 609, Fort Erie, Ontario L2A 5X3

Not valid for current subscribers to Love Inspired Suspense larger-print books.

**Are you a current subscriber to Love Inspired Suspense books
and want to receive the larger-print edition?
Call 1-800-873-8635 or visit www.ReaderService.com.**

* Terms and prices subject to change without notice. Prices do not include applicable taxes. Sales tax applicable in N.Y. Canadian residents will be charged applicable taxes. Offer not valid in Quebec. This offer is limited to one order per household. All orders subject to credit approval. Credit or debit balances in a customer's account(s) may be offset by any other outstanding balance owed by or to the customer. Please allow 4 to 6 weeks for delivery. Offer available while quantities last.

Your Privacy—The Reader Service is committed to protecting your privacy. Our Privacy Policy is available online at www.ReaderService.com or upon request from the Reader Service.

We make a portion of our mailing list available to reputable third parties that offer products we believe may interest you. If you prefer that we not exchange your name with third parties, or if you wish to clarify or modify your communication preferences, please visit us at www.ReaderService.com/consumerschoice or write to us at Reader Service Preference Service, P.O. Box 9062, Buffalo, NY 14269. Include your complete name and address.

LISUSLP11B